Summer Vows With A Detroit Gangsta

KYIRIS ASHLEY

U.A.D PRESENTS

Stay Up to Date

To stay up to date on new releases, plus get information on contests, sneak peeks and more,

Click the link below...
https://mailchi.mp/6d21003686d1/subscribe

Soundtracks

Scan the QR Code below to listen to the Soundtracks/Singles of some of your favorite U.A.D titles:

Don't have Spotify or Apple Music?
No Sweat!
Visit your choice streaming platform and search URBAN AINT DEAD.

Currently on lock serving a bid?
JPay, iHeartRadio, WHATEVER!
We got you covered.
Simply log into your facility's kiosk or tablet, go to music and search
URBAN AINT DEAD.

U.A.D PRESENTS

Like & Follow us on social media:

FB - URBAN AINT DEAD

IG: @uadpresents

Tik Tok - @uadpresents

Submission Guidelines

Submit the first three chapters of your completed manuscript to urbanaintdead@gmail.com, subject line: Your book's title. The manuscript must be in a .doc file and sent as an attachment. The document should be in Times New Roman, double-spaced, and in size 12 font. Also, provide your synopsis and full contact information. If sending multiple submissions, they must each be in a separate email. Have a story but no way to submit it electronically? You can still submit to URBAN AINT DEAD. Send in the first three chapters, written or typed, of your completed manuscript to:

URBAN AINT DEAD
P.O Box 448
Maybrook, NY 12543

DO NOT send original manuscript. Must be a duplicate.
Provide your synopsis and a cover letter containing your full contact information.
Thanks for considering URBAN AINT DEAD.

Wednesday

Chapter One

THE SCENT of lavender and fresh linen still lingered in the air, mingling with the warm breeze slipping through the cracked bedroom window. Morning sunbeams danced across Serenity's skin as she slowly opened her eyes. Her legs were tangled with Reason's beneath the sheets. For a moment, she just laid there, enjoying the quiet peace of her home. Reason wrapped his arm around her, pulling her in close before kissing the nape of her neck. She smiled, weaving her fingers between his. She hadn't been laying there for a full five minutes when she heard the tiny footsteps running down the hall before the bedroom door creaked open.

"I'm hungry!" Scotland's little voice called out.

"Me too!" Easton added.

Serenity smiled against the pillow, her heart blooming like it did every morning in this house. Reason groaned beside her and reached up to rub his eyes, the thin chain around his neck glinting in the sunlight.

"Your kids up early again," he mumbled, voice thick with sleep.

Serenity leaned up on one elbow, her long curls tumbling over her shoulder. "*Our* kids. And it's almost nine. They let us sleep in this morning."

Reason cracked one eye open and smirked. "You tryna make breakfast?"

"Yeah, I can hook a little somethin' up." She grinned and kissed his cheek before slipping out of bed.

Serenity walked down the stairs and went right to the kitchen. She tied her robe at the waist, turned on the Bluetooth speaker, and let the soft voice of Summer Walker fill the kitchen. It was the playlist she'd made for the weekend. Four days of love, family, and celebration was already working its magic. A wedding they'd spent an entire year planning would now take place in just a few days. Serenity smiled, thinking how she would soon officially be Mrs. Alexander.

She pulled out eggs, thick-cut bacon, and a can of biscuits. While the oven preheated, she cut up ripe peaches and strawberries for a fruit bowl, singing along to the music as she worked. The kids had started bickering over cartoons in the living room, but Serenity didn't mind. This was home. This was her second chance at love, and she loved the way her story had been rewritten.

The death of Scotland's father had shattered her heart, and she'd felt like she would never love again. The loss of him taught Serenity to guard her heart, and that was something she'd been doing until Reason wheeled himself in her office that day. From that day forward, their love had blossomed into the most beautiful love Serenity had ever experienced. Now here she was, just a few days shy of being his wife. She glanced up as Reason walked into the kitchen, shirtless and still sleepy. Easton was on his hip, and Scotland was trailing behind.

"Smells good in here," he said, kissing her cheek.

"You look good in here," she replied, eyes roaming him slowly.

He set Easton down and stepped behind her, wrapping his arms around her waist while she flipped bacon in the skillet. She leaned into him, feeling the weight of him behind her.

"You ready?" he whispered.

Serenity's heart thumped in her chest. It was not because she was unsure but because she *was*. "More than ever," she whispered. "I still can't believe I get to marry you. I'm going to make you so happy."

Reason didn't speak for a second. He just held her, kissed her neck once, then went to pour the kids some juice. Once the food was done, Serenity made the kids' plates first, being sure to add apple jelly to Scotland's biscuit and strawberry to Easton's. Reason took their plates to the table while Serenity made one for her and him. Once they were all at the table, Serenity couldn't help but smile at the way her life had changed.

The kitchen was filled with laughter and mayhem. Scotland spilled her juice twice, while Easton demanded seconds. However, Serenity moved through it all gracefully, helping each of the children with their needs all while singing along to H.E.R. Reason leaned against the counter, watching her with a soft, unreadable smile. This was his peace – this house, this woman, and these two wild children that somehow became *his*.

Reason glanced at the time, noticing that it was now almost eleven. "Alright, I gotta go get dressed, so I can head to the airport."

It was the Wednesday before the wedding, and family from out of town had begun rolling in. First to arrive were Reason's play cousins from Texas. They grew up right alongside Reason and Ace when they were kids up until the twins' parents moved them to Texas when they were fifteen. Even though they were hundreds of miles away, they still kept in touch with each family visiting the other at least once a year. They would be the only family Reason had at his wedding; the day he was going to marry the love of his life. He wished Peaches was there to see how far he'd come, the healing that had taken place which he knew was all because of Serenity. He knew his mother was smiling down on him, and that kept him going.

Reason hadn't seen his cousins in several years. They'd been locked up, finishing a five-year bid when Peaches passed away, so they weren't even able to come up for the funeral. However, the moment they found out about Reason getting married, they booked the first flight to Detroit.

"What time does their fight land?" Serenity asked, wiping jelly off Easton's chin.

"It lands in twenty minutes, so I gotta hurry up. I'm the one told them not to rent a car, so I can't have them waiting."

"I can't wait to meet them."

Reason grinned. "They been ready to meet you too."

He kissed her forehead before heading up into his en-suite bathroom to shower before getting dressed. Reason was casual, dressed in a black tee and a pair of jeans. Yet his diamond-studded Rolex and Cartier frames added just what he needed to his look. There was a time when

Reason thought he would never walk again, never be happy again, or even want to live. But that was all behind him. Serenity had made sure of that. She'd come in and made Reason completely forget about every past love that didn't work, all the heartache he'd been through, and all of the loss he suffered. None of that mattered anymore, and it was all because of Serenity's love.

Reason walked out the house, and the sun beamed down on him. It wasn't even noon yet, and it was already in the high seventies, so Reason knew it would be a hot day in the city. He got inside his Tesla SUV before making his way to Detroit Metro Airport.

The automatic doors slid open, and there they stood. Valor and Vice, the Everhart twins from Dallas, were impossible to ignore. Six-foot-five and cut from pure Black royalty, they walked through baggage claim, heads held high, catching smiles from each woman they passed. Valor, the older twin by three minutes, had smooth brown skin, broad shoulders, and waves so deep they could make you seasick if you looked too long. His full beard connected like it had been sculpted. He wore a crisp black button-up that was slightly unbuttoned at the top, revealing his thick Cuban link chain. His jeans were dark, tailored, and clean. On his feet were a fresh pair of Prada sneakers. The diamond crusted Rolex he wore gleamed every time the light hit it.

Vice was the wild one. He had long locs that were neat and twisted to perfection and deep-set hazel eyes. Tattoos peeked from beneath his crisp white tee, running down to his arms all the way to his knuckles. Gold grills gleamed every time he grinned, and his chain swung low with a lion pendant that used to belong to their late father. Where Valor gave "smooth operator", Vice gave "don't play with me".

Reason stepped out his SUV, ready to see his cousins. "Texas done touched down," he said with a smirk.

"And we ready for the weekend." Valor nodded, pulling Reason in for a hug.

"Detroit 'bout to be on fire this weekend," Vice added, tossing his duffle in the trunk.

"Y'all ain't bring no drama, right?" Reason asked.

Valor smirked. "Only the good kind."

They laughed, climbed into Reason's SUV, and peeled off from the curb. They drove through the streets, all ready to start the weekend festivities. They hadn't been together like this in years. So, they all knew that a time was going to be had.

"I gotta go make a small detour, and then we can go to my house," Reason informed. The twins agreed, sitting back and enjoying the ride.

Reason pulled up at a two-story brick home on the eastside of Detroit about thirty minutes later. "I'ma be right back, two seconds."

"That's cool but be quick. We not strapped, and we already know how the eastside of Detroit gets down." Valor looked into the sideview mirror. He saw a crackhead standing at the corner.

Reason jumped out the car, jogging to the door. Valor stayed on high alert, keeping his head on a swivel. He saw a black car pull up a few houses down and park, but no one got out. The windows had dark tint, so he couldn't see who was inside. Valor pointed the car out to Vice, wanting him to be ready for anything. Although neither of them had a gun, their hands still worked, and they would use them if need be. Before the person in the car could make a move, Valor saw Reason jogging back to the SUV with a black duffle bag in hand. Valor kept his eyes on the car, and the window rolled down halfway just as Reason passed by. When the car didn't follow them, Valor let it go, sitting back in his seat as Reason drove to his house.

Chapter Two

S ERENITY HAD JUST GOTTEN out the shower and put on a robe before walking out into the hallway. The sunlight poured through the sheer curtains as she moved between the kids' rooms with her usual quiet rhythm. She laid out Scotland's outfit first on her pale pink comforter, a white cotton romper with flutter sleeves and tiny embroidered strawberries paired with red sandals and a matching bow for her hair. She tucked her favorite doll beside it and smiled to herself. Then, she stepped into Easton's room, laying a cool mint green polo and khaki shorts across his bed with little black Nike slides sitting underneath. She called both of the children into their rooms and told them to get dressed before walking back to her room.

She pulled open the closet and chose a butter-yellow two-piece linen set with high-waisted shorts that hugged her hips just right and a cropped, sleeveless, wrap top that tied in the back. The outfit kissed her curves without trying too hard, showing off the honey glow of her skin. She stepped into gold flat sandals, picking out gold jewelry and a gold purse to match.

At her vanity, she swept her long curls into a soft, low ponytail and swooped her edges carefully. She brushed a little bronzer on her cheekbones, lined her lips with cocoa brown, and filled them in with a soft nude gloss. Finally, she sprayed on Creed Love in White all over her body.

She caught a glimpse of herself in the mirror and let out a soft, breathy laugh. "I'm really about to be somebody's wife," she whispered, voice thick with emotion.

However, Serenity knew she wasn't marrying just anyone. She was marrying Reason Alexander, a man who had every reason to shut down after what he'd been through but chose instead to open up to her, a man who had touched every dark part of her and filled it with light, a man who made her feel safe, seen, wanted, but most of all, loved.

It was a second chance at real love and the first chance to feel things she'd never felt before. Where Reason thought Serenity healed him, Serenity knew Reason healed her. He'd come in and not only loved her but her daughter as well. He was a true leader to the family they were building. For that, she would be eternally grateful and would be sure to show it every day.

Serenity stepped into the kitchen one last time, checking the overnight bag she'd packed for the kids. Extra clothes, pajamas, snacks, iPads, everything was there. Her nerves were buzzing with excitement, but her mind was already on the meeting she had scheduled in less than an hour, the approval of the custom floral arrangements for the reception centerpieces. Serenity needed everything to be perfect for her special day, and she'd been working hard to ensure everything was. Two of her cousins had already RSVP'd with plus ones they weren't supposed to have, causing her to reset the entire seating chart. So, she didn't need any more surprises.

She also had to meet with her wedding planner, Amira, at the venue to do a final walkthrough. After slipping her phone and gloss into a mini crossbody, Serenity called out to the kids, letting them know it was time to go. Scotland came running first, dressed and beaming. Easton followed a second later, dragging a small backpack behind him like he was going on an adventure.

The sun beat down on her parents' brick home, and Serenity felt a wave of comfort the moment she pulled into the driveway. The flower beds were still perfect, the screen door creaked the same, and the smell of her mama's lemon pound cake hit her the second they stepped inside the house.

"Look who's here!" her mother called from the kitchen, wiping her hands on a dish towel.

Scotland and Easton ran into their grandparents' arms, while Serenity spotted her sister sitting at the dining room table, barefaced and beautiful in a Detroit vs Everybody tee, sipping iced coffee like she had nothing in the world to do.

"You look too cute, sista," she spoke, looking over at Serenity. "Where you headed?"

Serenity smiled. "Final meeting with Amira and some more wedding stuff."

Shayla stood, grabbing her purse. "I'm coming. Somebody gotta keep you from overthinking everything."

Serenity laughed. "I'm not overthinking."

"Girl, you changed the linen napkin color *three* times."

"Okay. So what? I got it right the last time though."

"Bitch, it was fine the first time."

Stephanie chuckled from the kitchen before walking over to her daughter. "Y'all sound just like y'all did when y'all were teenagers trying to plan that backyard party me and y'all daddy let y'all have."

Shayla laughed and smiled at her mother.

Serenity leaned over and kissed her mom's cheek. "Thank you for keeping the kids."

"You go do bride stuff." Stephanie smiled. "Me and your dad will hold it down here."

Serenity and Shayla pulled off, windows down and music up, enjoying the warm breeze and beautiful weather.

"You really about to be a wife," Shayla spoke with a soft grin.

Serenity looked over at her and smiled. "Yeah. I really am. I'm going to be a wonderful wife to an extraordinary man."

"I know that's right, sis, go off. Where is Reason anyway?"

"He had to go pick up his twin cousins from the airport. They flew in from Texas today."

"Twin cousins? Bitch, why I ain't never heard about them? I hear that everything's bigger in Texas," Shayla only half joked.

"I've never met them. They moved to Texas when they were in their teens and were both locked up when I met Reason."

"Oh, yeah, I need to meet them. I'm trying to find my Mr. Right Now, and he just might be at yo wedding."

"Oh, hell nah. There will be no fucking family at my wedding. This is a classy event, not a trailer park barbeque." Serenity chuckled before turning the music up.

About twenty minutes later, Serenity and Shayla were pulling into a parking space. The air inside the floral studio was cool and fragrant, filled with the soft sound of jazz music and the subtle rustle of stems being trimmed behind the counter. Serenity and Shayla walked in together, walking effortlessly across the polished floors. They were greeted immediately by their florist, **Anika**, a petite brown skinned woman with silver locs.

"You're right on time, Serenity," Anika said, waving them over. "Everything's prepped and ready for your final approval."

Serenity smiled politely, ready to see the arrangements. This was one of the last pieces of her dream wedding, so the floral design had to be perfect. Anika led them into a back room where several arrangements were displayed on pedestals, and a mockup of the altar was set up under soft studio lighting.

Serenity's breath caught in her throat. The flower arrangements were breathtaking. Tall, cascading arrangements of cream roses, peach peonies, and taupe hydrangeas stood like art. Ivory orchids were draped over the sides in soft, romantic folds, accented with sprigs of golden eucalyptus and blush gardenias. The taupe-toned ribbons tied around the bases added a soft, neutral elegance that perfectly balanced the warmth of the peach and the softness of the cream.

"Oh, my God," Shayla whispered. "This is magazine cover-level fine."

Serenity stepped closer and reached out to touch one of the petals, overwhelmed by how real it was all starting to feel.

"This is exactly what I pictured," she said. "I love it. I absolutely love it."

"Yeah, sis, this is really beautiful," Shayla added.

"Then we're locked in. Everything will be delivered and set up Saturday morning just as we discussed." Anika beamed.

"Perfect. Thank you so much, Anika. This is beautiful. More than I even expected." Serenity walked up to the front of the flower shop, pulling her card from her purse and making the final payment on her flowers. When she was done, they walked back to the car, heading to the next stop.

<hr>

By the time Serenity and Shayla pulled up to The Detroit Grand, a luxury waterfront venue tucked near the edge of downtown, the city was glowing under the thick, golden summer sun. Serenity stepped out and paused, eyes running across the elegant stone steps, the wrought-iron gates, and the soft breeze coming off the river. Inside, the wedding planner, Amira, waited with her iPad and signature headset, ready to command.

"Hey, bride-to-be," Amira said, giving her a quick hug. "You ready for the walkthrough?"

"Sure am. Let's do it," Serenity replied.

They moved from room to room – the bridal suite, the ceremony terrace with rows of ivory Chiavari chairs, and the glass ballroom where the reception would take place. The sunlight flooded in through floor-to-ceiling windows, making the floors glow like honey. Amira walked her through table placement, music transitions, cake staging, and timeline flow. Shayla nodded along, taking mental notes but mostly just soaking it in.

"You did that, sis," Shayla whispered. "This is dream wedding level."

Serenity smiled, nodding her head, agreeing with Shayla. That was until her phone started buzzing in her purse. She glanced at the screen to see Shane's face flashing across it. Serenity had left Shane in charge of the clinic for the two weeks she'd taken off for the wedding. This was only his first day running it, and he was already calling.

She answered quickly. "Shane? What's up? Is everything okay?"

His voice was filled with panic. "*Serenity, the clinic's on fire.*"

Serenity froze, not believing what Shane had just said to her. "What?"

"I don't know how it started. One of the neighbors called it in. The back office is already gone. It's bad, Serenity."

Her free hand went to her chest.

Shayla immediately stepped in. "What's wrong, sis?"

Serenity's eyes locked on hers. "The clinic. It's on fire."

Amira paused mid-sentence, sensing the shift.

Shane's voice came through again. "The fire department's here, but it's spreading fast. They said it looked intentional."

Serenity's mind raced. That clinic was her life's work. Her dream after her grandmother passed was to be a physical therapist, and she had built her clinic from the ground up. She'd put her blood, sweat, and tears into that place, and now it was in flames.

———

BY THE TIME Serenity and Shayla pulled up to the clinic, thick plumes of black smoke curled into the sky like a warning shot. The brick building she'd once poured her heart into with late-night shifts, early-morning rounds, and too many tears to count was now engulfed in flames. Fire trucks surrounded the lot, red lights swirling over chaos as firefighters worked to control the blaze. The back half of the building was already caved in, scorched to the bone. Windows were blown out. Ash and heat filled the air, coating Serenity's skin like a second, bitter layer of grief.

"No..." Serenity whispered as she tried to run to her clinic, hand over her mouth.

Shayla reached for her. "Don't run up, sis. Let the firefighters do their job."

Serenity's feet were already moving, slow and dazed, across the pavement. The heat hit her like a wave, forcing her to stop near the barricade tape as a firefighter stepped in front of her.

"Ma'am, I'm gonna need you to stand back."

"This is my clinic," she said, voice cracking. "I own this building." She didn't cry, not yet. She just stared as the fire devoured what was left of all her hard work. This one building held so many memories. She remembered when Scotland's father gave her the money to build it. She remembered how heartbroken she was when he was murdered before it was finished. She remembered the first day Reason wheeled himself into her office. There were so many memories, and they were all going up in smoke.

"Serenity!" Shane called out, running over to her.

Serenity fell into Shane's arms, hugging him tightly. "Are you okay? Did everyone make it out the building?"

"Yeah, everyone is fine. Thankfully, there were no patients in the clinic at the time. We were about to go to lunch when I heard the smoke detectors going off. When I went to check, one of the rooms were fully engulfed in flames. I damn near scuffed my Fendi loafers trying to run out that damn building."

"This is awful. Who would do this?" Shayla asked.

Serenity shook her head, numb to it all. "I don't know... but they didn't just burn a building. They burned down memories too."

Shane held Serenity as she cried, while Shayla pulled out her phone and called Reason. "You need to come to the clinic. It's on fire. She's here, and it's bad."

Reason hung up before Shayla could say another word. Not even ten minutes later, Reason's SUV was coming down the street. He pulled up fast, dust kicking behind his tires. He jumped out first and rushed over to Serenity, wrapping his arms around her. Valor and Vice stepped out behind him, both surveying the scene.

"You okay? Were you inside when it happened?" he asked in a low tone.

"Nah, I was at the venue when Shane called me." Tears fell from Serenity's eyes. "Someone set my clinic on fire, and I don't know why."

Reason didn't respond, just held her tighter, knowing that he would build her another one twice the size. His main focus was finding out who did this and why. Serenity shouldn't have any enemies, so he didn't understand how any of this could be happening.

"Baby, why do you think someone set the clinic on fire? You sure this wasn't just an accident?"

"The firemen told Shane it was intentional. Someone started this fire, and I don't know why."

Tears fell from Serenity's eyes like flowing rivers, and Reason's anger grew. He hated seeing Serenity cry, so he vowed to always keep a smile on her face. This was supposed to be one of the happiest times in Serenity's life, and someone was trying to ruin it. Reason wasn't having that.

Whoever is behind this shit is going to pay with their life, Reason vowed to himself.

Valor stood still at the edge of the lot, his eyes narrowing. Across the street, parked just far enough to avoid attention, was a black Chrysler 300 with dark tinted windows. It was the same car he'd noticed earlier at Reason's spot.

"Yo," he said under his breath, nudging Vice. "That's the same ride from earlier."

Vice turned, chewing his lip. "Yeah? You sure?"

"Positive."

The car didn't move, just sat there like it was watching. A chill crawled up Valor's spine. He knew how this shit worked. This was no random fire. Somebody sent a message. And now, whoever was in that car might be waiting to see how the message landed.

Valor's jaw clenched. "We need to let Reason know. Something ain't right about this shit."

Just as Valor turned to walk toward Reason, the car pulled off down the street. The car slowly moved past them, letting Valor and Vice know the driver had indeed been watching. Something told Valor this wouldn't be the last time they would see that black Chrysler. He walked up to Reason just as he was telling Serenity to get into the car. He watched as another woman and a white man walked with her.

"Yo, this ain't some random shit. I wasn't gon' to say shit at first because I thought it wasn't nothing. But when we pulled up to yo spot earlier, I saw a black car just watching. Then, just now, I saw that same black car."

Reason shook his head. He didn't know what the fuck was going on. Everyone Reason thought would want to do something so horrible, everyone Reason had beef with, was dead – or so he thought.

Chapter Three

Kilo arrived at his home on the eastside about thirty minutes later. He walked to his kitchen, grabbing a beer before heading downstairs. He took a seat, leaning back in the cracked leather chair in his basement hideout. The glow from the single hanging bulb was the only light in the entire basement. Sweat trickled down the side of his neck, not from heat but from the high. From *satisfaction*.

He'd made it back just in time to catch the news. "*Local clinic engulfed in flames*, still under investigation." The reporter hadn't said Serenity's name, but Kilo didn't need confirmation. He knew the building. Knew who it mattered to. Knew exactly what kind of message it would send. He lit a blunt and took a long drag, exhaling slowly.

"This for you, Brick," he muttered, eyes fixed on the TV. "I told you I'd make somebody bleed for what they did."

He was going to get revenge for his brother's death, no matter how long it took. Brick didn't deserve to die, and he was going to make sure Reason paid for the part he played in Brick's death. He didn't care how many bodies he had to drop before he got to Reason. Everyone standing in the way had to die. Kilo had spent an entire year plaining, and it was now time to put everything into motion.

"Burnin' that little clinic down was just the beginning," Kilo said, jaw tight. "I want him to feel it first. Want him to know that someone is gunnin' for him. I want him to watch it all fall down around him before I take him out. Ain't no gettin' married. Ain't no happy ending."

He opened the drawer beside him and pulled out a black and white photo of Reason and Ace back in their younger days, thick as thieves. He drew a fat red X through Ace's face then circled Reason's.

"This time, I'm takin' my time," he said, tapping ash into a tray shaped like a pistol. "I want it done *right*."

He picked up his phone and sent a short message to Chrome.

Kilo: It's on tomorrow

Reason had gotten a whole new crew. Everyone had been replaced except for Chrome. Reason didn't know they were cousins. And since Reason thought he could still trust Chrome, he kept him around. It was good for Kilo because through Chrome, he was able to keep an eye on Reason's every move.

Kilo finished his beer and blunt, watching the news until it went off. The air was thick with weed smoke forming a cloud around him. The fire at Serenity's clinic was just a whisper, just a taste of the war he planned to finish. Because Ace may have been gone, laid out cold and six feet deep, but Reason was still breathing. Still walking around Detroit like the city belonged to him. Like Brick's murder didn't mean shit to him.

Brick had been more than a brother to Kilo. He'd been his backbone, the only one who ever had his back when the world turned cold. When Reason put a price on Brick's head, he didn't just take a soldier. He split Kilo's life in half. Now, Reason was days away from getting married, throwing parties, laughing, and living his best life, and that was a problem for Kilo.

Kilo crossed the room and opened his gun closet. It was an old steel locker that he had bolted into the foundation. He twisted the key, pulled the handle, and the metal groaned as it opened wide. Inside was a *small arsenal*. The first one he grabbed was his Glock 19. It had a tan frame and an extended mag already loaded. He checked the chamber, pulled the slide back, then let it snap forward with a heavy click.

Next came the FN SCAR, matte black with a custom scope and silencer. He had plans for that one. That would lead his way into the party, chopping up everyone in his line of fire. Then, there was the Draco, short barrel and compact but loud as hell. This was a streetsweeper, no finesse, just chaos. Kilo loaded it, set it on the table beside him, and continued going through his guns.

On the second shelf sat his pride and joy, a custom 1911, polished chrome with a pearl handle. It had Brick's name etched into the slide. This one was personal. This was for the final shot, the one that would end Reason. Clip after clip, he stacked hollow points into magazines like it was therapy. Each round clicked in sounded like music to Kilo's ears.

By the time he finished, the table beside him was full with enough ammo to wage a small war. He pulled a black duffle from under the table and started placing everything inside. When he was done, he walked upstairs and placed his bag at the door then poured himself a glass of Hennessy. He sat back on his couch, staring at the wall where an old photo of Brick hung in a crooked frame. Brick, with his shirt off, was throwing up the set with wild eyes and that signature grin. It was the only photo Kilo had of his brother, and he would hang that picture in his living room no matter where he lived.

"I got you, bro," Kilo said under his breath. "Ain't no happy ending for that nigga. Not while I'm still breathing."

His phone buzzed on the table, and he saw it was one of his lookouts.

"They all back at the house. He got some twins with him. I ain't never seen these niggas before," Reco spoke into the phone.

Kilo's lips twisted. "Yeah, I know. I seen them nigga earlier today. It don't matter though. Them niggas can get it too. Let them niggas breathe tonight. We gonna fuck shit up tomorrow at that rehearsal dinner."

Kilo knew that tomorrow was going to start a fire that wouldn't get put out with water. He didn't care about wedding vows, flower girls, or family coming in from out of state. He cared about making Reason feel every bit of what he'd lost. And when it was time, when they were all distracted by champagne and music, he'd strike. He finished his drink and went to take a shower.

Tomorrow, he'd blend in with the city. Show up where they least expected him. And if Reason Alexander thought he was walking into forever this weekend, Kilo was ready to make sure *he didn't walk out at all.*

Tʜᴀᴛ ɴɪɢʜᴛ, Reason and Serenity made their way back home. The ride was quiet, the weight of the day still hanging over them like a thundercloud. Valor and Vice rode in the backseat, silent but alert, eyes sharp in the dark. Serenity had been too shaken to drive, so Shayla drove Serenity's car back to their parents' house. Reason would just take her to get it when she was ready.

Parking in their driveway, Reason turned to look at Serenity in the passenger seat. Her eyes were swollen, her hands folded in her lap like she was trying to hold herself together. Without a word, he reached over and squeezed her thigh gently.

"Come on, baby. Let's go in the house so that I can run you a bubble bath."

Serenity let out a long sigh before slowly opening the door. Reason could see how sad Serenity was, and he hated it. She should be smiling the night before their rehearsal dinner, but instead, she walked inside the house with tear filled eyes. She walked directly up to their bedroom, while Reason showed Valor and Vice their guest suites on the lower level, both stocked with fresh towels and toiletries. Valor gave a quiet nod of thanks. Vice cracked a joke to lighten the mood but fell silent when he looked at Reason's face. It wasn't the time for jokes.

Reason walked back to his bedroom, seeing Serenity standing at the window, looking out into the darkness. He could see the tears rolling down her face in her refection, and his heart broke. He knew how much the clinic meant to Serenity, and even with him building her another one, he knew it would never be the same. A soft, choked sob escaped her lips, and Reason rushed to her. He wrapped his arms around her tightly, holding her against his chest.

"I put everything into that clinic," she whispered. "My whole purpose in life was to heal people, and now, my clinic is gone."

"It's still your purpose, baby. I promise you're going to have a new clinic in no time. I know that clinic meant everything to you, so it meant everything to me. I promise I will have you another one built, and you will be back to work in no time."

She turned around slowly, burying her face into his chest. He held her tighter.

"I swear to you, baby," Reason assured, pulling back just enough to look her in the eyes. "The next one is going to be bigger and better. I promise. You will have total control of the build. Anything you want, you can have. I got you, baby. I put that on everything I love."

She nodded, broken but believing him. Because if there was one thing she knew about Reason Alexander, it was that he would move heaven and earth for her. When he made a promise, he meant it. Reason would go to war for Serenity, and she knew it.

Reason ran Serenity a hot bubble bath, lighting candles all around the bathroom. He placed her MacBook on her bath shelf before going to the kitchen for a bottle of wine and a glass. He poured her wine before setting the glass and bottle on the shelf next to her laptop. Once Serenity was in the tub and Reason made sure she was okay, he walked down to his office. He had calls to make. His first order of business was finding out who'd set Serenity's clinic on fire.

He called his crew, telling them to put the word out, twenty-five thousand to whoever could find the person who'd done it. Reason had no clue who could have done this. To his knowledge, everyone he had beef with was dead. However, if someone had beef with Serenity, then he would be he one to handle it. He went to sleep that night holding Serenity close.

Thursday

Chapter Four

The house was quiet for the first time in what felt like forever. The sun crept through the blinds without the sound of tiny footsteps trailing behind it. There were no cartoons blaring from a tablet, no calls of "Mommy!" from down the hall. Just silence and birds outside the window. Serenity stirred first, blinking against the light shining in her eyes. Her body was wrapped in the soft warmth of their bed and the even warmer strength of Reason's arms around her waist. His breath was steady against the back of her neck, his chest rising and falling in sync with hers.

Her heart was still bruised, but today was her rehearsal dinner. It was a joyous occasion, and she wasn't going to let anything get in the way of that. She shifted slowly, careful not to wake Reason just yet, and stared at the ceiling for a long moment. Her eyes burned again, but she blinked the tears away. Today wasn't about what was lost. It was about what she was gaining. In just forty-eight hours, she would walk down the aisle and marry the man who held her through every breakdown, who kissed every scar, who reminded her she still had a future. She exhaled slowly and slipped out of bed.

Reason stirred almost immediately. "You good?" His voice was low and heavy with sleep.

She turned to him with a faint smile. "Yeah. Just getting me some of this quiet. You know we don't get it often."

He smirked. "No kids jumping on the bed this morning. Shit, I must still be dreamin'."

Serenity climbed back onto the edge of the bed, brushing his cheek with the backs of her fingers. "Well, get used to it because my parents keeping them until we come back from the honeymoon. I gotta pack them a bag, so I can take it with us to the rehearsal dinner."

"Damn near two weeks kid free? Shit, a nigga ain't gon' know how to act." Reason laughed, reaching for her hand and bringing it to his lips. He kissed her knuckles gently then looked up at her. "You still sad?"

She hesitated then nodded. "A little. But I'm trying to let that go. At least for the next few days. I want to be present, you know? This is the beginning of forever."

Reason sat up and pulled her into his lap. She curled into him like second nature. "I told you last night," he said, pressing a kiss to her shoulder, "you're not losin' nothin'. We gon' rebuild everything they tried to take. And this time, it's gon' be bigger and better."

She smiled into his neck, eyes glassy. "You always know how to say the right thing."

"Nah," he whispered. "I just say what I mean."

They sat in silence for a beat, wrapped in the quiet comfort of each other. No phones, no interruptions, no drama, just them. A few moments later, Serenity exhaled and pushed herself to her feet. "Alright," she spoke, voice lighter. "Today is about love, coordination, and making sure my cousin, Karma, doesn't show up late to the rehearsal. That bitch is late for everything."

Reason laughed and stretched. "She wanna move on her own time. It's cool just as long as she's not late for the wedding."

Reason had only met Karma one other time since he'd been with Serenity. She lived in Ohio and didn't come back home much. She was Serenity's favorite cousin and cool as hell. Reason was happy she was in town and hoped that seeing her would cheer Serenity up.

Serenity smirked, already walking toward the bathroom. "If she late for the wedding, that bitch is not eating at the reception."

Reason laughed as he watched her disappear into the bathroom, the sound of running water following a moment later. For a second, Reason closed his eyes and let the peace sink in. He knew it wouldn't last long. He'd already put word out in the streets, so he knew shit was about to go down. However, for now, he was going to enjoy this peace.

By the time Serenity stepped out of the steamy bathroom, wrapped in a white towel with her skin glowing and her curls pinned up to air dry, her mood had shifted, her sadness washed away by the shower. Although her heart was still healing, Serenity refused to let sadness follow her into this next chapter. Today, she was showing up in love, style, and power. She walked into both of the kids' rooms, packing them both a bag with enough clothes to last them the next two weeks.

Back in the master bedroom, laid out across the tufted bench at the foot of the bed, were the outfits she and Reason had agreed on for today's ceremony run-through. The wedding colors – taupe, peach, and cream – were weaved into their looks flawlessly. Serenity slipped into a silk, cream-colored wrap dress that clung to her curves like it was tailor made for her. It featured a deep v-neckline and subtle pleats at the waist, flowing just above the knee with an elegant slit along the side. Soft, peach-toned strappy heels wrapped around her ankles like satin ribbons. She added gold hoops, a matching bracelet, and a peach and cream clutch shaped like a flower.

She sat at her vanity and applied her makeup, a soft-glam that was beat to perfection, flawless dewy skin, a taupe smoky eye, and glossy nude lips. However, the finishing touch was her scent. She reached for the sleek white and gold bottle on her vanity, Nishane's Hundred Silent Ways. It had been one of her go to fragrances for the last few weeks. The notes of peach and white flowers mixed with creamy vanilla made it perfect for summer. She sprayed it behind her ears, between her thighs, the base of her neck, her wrists and ankles, knowing that her second chance at love deserved a scent worthy of being remembered.

Meanwhile, Reason stood in front of the mirror in the master bathroom, buttoning up a custom-fitted taupe linen shirt with cream piping along the cuffs and collar. The shirt was pressed crisp, overlapping a pair of cream trousers, cuffed at the ankles to show off his tan designer loafers. He wore his gold Cuban link chain tucked beneath the shirt, only a hint peeking from the open top buttons. His wrist rocked a brushed gold Audemars Piguet. He took his time placing a single diamond stud in his ear. His waves were tight, and his beard was lined to perfection.

Reason was stepping out. This wasn't just a rehearsal; it was the first time both of their families would be in the same room together. Reason reached for the matte black bottle from the top bathroom shelf, Fragrance du Bois Oud Jaune Intense. The scent was laced with luxury. The fragrance was oud, vanilla, and musk on the dry down, however opened with top notes of pineapple and ylang-ylang, making it a perfect scent for the occasion. He sprayed himself before looking in the mirror once more.

"Damn." Serenity smiled, stepping into the doorway, looking him over. "My man looks good as hell," she complimented

Reason smiled, looking over at Serenity. "Shit, you look like I already said I do." Reason wrapped his arms around Serenity's waist. Serenity smiled before leaning into his chest. "I can't wait to make you Mrs. Alexander."

Serenity smiled. "And I can't wait to be your wife. Are you ready to start forever with me?"

"I been ready. Now, let's get outta here before we're late to our own rehearsal. I'ma take the kids' bags to the car."

Serenity nodded her head, smiling as she watched Reason walk out the room. She looked at herself once more in the full-length mirror in the corner of the room, making sure everything was perfect. When she saw it indeed was, she was ready to walk out the door.

The rehearsal was scheduled for 2:00 p.m. sharp at The Detroit Grand, the luxurious riverfront venue where Serenity and Reason would say "I do" in just forty-eight hours. When the Tesla pulled up with their small convoy of cars behind it, the staff members were already waiting at the private entrance to usher them in.

Inside, the event space was transformed into a soft dreamscape of taupe, peach, and cream. Rows of ivory Chiavari chairs were arranged on the terrace overlooking the water. The floral designer had left a sample arrangement at the front, peach peonies, cream roses, and taupe hydrangeas rising from the gold pedestal like a romantic promise in full bloom. The wedding planner, Amira, stood, clipboard in hand, headset on, already directing ushers, bridesmaids, and groomsmen into their designated areas.

Serenity stepped into the space with a tight inhale. Even though it was a rehearsal, everything felt so *real* now. Her eyes scanned the aisle, and for a second, she imagined the music, the whispers of guests, and Reason waiting for her at the altar. Her heart fluttered.

"Alright, y'all," Amira called. "Let's line up!"

The bridal party fell into formation. Serenity's maid of honor, her sister, Shayla, took her place beside her. The bridesmaids followed, her cousin, Karma, and her two college roommates, Brielle and Nyla. On the other side, Reason's best man was his cousin, Vice The groomsmen followed after, Valor, Reek, new to his crew but cool as hell, and Shane. Serenity wanted him on her side, but Reason knew none of his groomsmen were going to walk down with him. So, to keep him in the wedding, Reason made him a groomsman. Scotland giggled as she practiced tossing faux petals from her little satin basket, while Easton practiced holding the ring pillow like it was a priceless treasure.

"Keep it together, lil man," Vice joked, crouching to give him a fist bump. "You got a job to do in two days."

Easton puffed out his chest. "I'm gon' be ready."

Amira walked them all through the ceremony flow twice – entrances, music cues, where to stand, and when to exit. Serenity and Reason walked the aisle together last, holding hands, eyes locked. At the altar, Amira stepped back and gave them a knowing smile.

"Take it in," she said softly. "Saturday is the day."

Serenity swallowed hard, her fingers tightening around Reason's.

"I'm ready," she whispered.

"Been ready," he replied.

Once the rehearsal was over, Reason put Scotland and Easton's bags inside Serenity's father's car before they all made their way to dinner. Reservations had been made weeks ago at one of Detroit's finest restaurants, Prime + Proper, an upscale, modern steakhouse known for their eighty-dollar steaks. The private dining room was reserved exclusively for the Alexander wedding party.

As they pulled up to the valet in a sleek line of luxury cars, they snapped photos, laughed, and buzzed with anticipation for the wedding to come. Inside, crystal chandeliers hung low over velvet seating and curved booths. The energy was intimate and indulgent, everything Serenity wanted. Reason led her through the front entrance with his hand at the small of her back.

"You good?" he asked softly.

She looked up at him, the memory of flames still tucked somewhere in the back of her mind, but it was overshadowed now by love and laughter.

"I'm perfect," she replied.

With that, they walked in, ready to dine like royalty.

Chapter Five

THE CITY WAS LIT with gold and neon as night fell over downtown Detroit. The skyline glowed behind Prime + Proper. Inside, the rehearsal dinner for the Alexander wedding was in full swing. Champagne flutes clinked, laughter echoed off marble, and the smell of garlic butter and aged beef invaded the air around them.

Outside, death was pulling up to the curb. Kilo sat in the back of a matte black SUV with the windows tinted. The engine purred low as they turned the corner and crept toward the side of the restaurant. His crew was silent, all of them dressed in dark jeans, hoodies, and gloves. Black masks were tucked under their chins, ready. In the front seat sat Roc, a lean, sharp-nosed hitter with eyes as black as his soul. Beside him was Tre-5, the youngest in the crew, eager and trigger-happy. Lil Jugg rode next to Kilo in the back. Jugg was short, wide, and grimy with gold teeth and a permanent twitch in his jaw.

"Y'all know what it is," Kilo spoke, voice cold and measured. "In and out. Don't stop till I say. Reason gotta feel this shit."

Roc grinned, checking his weapon. "We really bringing it to 'em on wedding weekend?"

"Damn right," Kilo replied. "He had something to do with Brick's death. Burnin' down her clinic was the message. This here? This the *lesson.*"

Reason sat at the head of the table, diamond glinting in his ear, drink in hand. Serenity was beside him, laughing with Shayla and Karma, while Easton nibbled on a plate of lobster mac. Scotland sat beside him, dipping a piece of steak into A1 sauce. Everyone was sitting around the table, enjoying good food and good laughs. Love was in the air, and everyone could feel it. Then, the glass shattered.

Boom! Boom! Boom!

Screams rang out as the first rounds tore through the window. A wine glass exploded on the table. Serenity and Shayla immediately grabbed Easton and Scotland and rushed under the table, covering them with their own bodies.

Reason's instincts snapped, clicking in instantly. "Stay down," he yelled, pulling his gun from his waistline.

Thankfully, Reason had given both Valor and Vice a strap, so they would feel better about being in the city. It was a good thing he did because this was the time when they needed them. Vice reached for his piece first, pulling a Glock from under his jacket. Valor grabbed Stephanie, shielding her, so she could crawl underneath a table, while reaching for the piece strapped to his ankle.

"We got shooters outside!" Vice shouted, firing toward the window.

The air inside was thick with smoke, screams, and shattered glass. Kilo, Tre-5, and Roc entered through the front door, guns in hand. People screamed and ran for cover, trying not to be hit by any of the stray bullets. Tre-5 came in first, firing wildly at the wedding party. Valor dropped him with three to the chest before he could get past the second table. Roc followed, but Reason had already flanked around behind the wine bar. When Roc turned to shoot at Vice, Reason popped up and lit him up, two to the ribs, one to the throat. Blood hit the white tablecloths like paint.

Reason saw Shane trying to crawl toward the back exit. A stray bullet caught him in the arm.

"Ahhhh, fuck!" he screamed, holding his arm in pain.

Serenity tried to reach him, but Shayla yanked her back, not wanting her sister to be the next one shot. Valor dragged Shane behind the host stand, his hand pressed against the wound. Serenity watched in fear, praying that all her loved ones made it out of this alive. Tears fell from her eyes as she gripped Easton tightly.

"Mommy, I'm scared," Scotland cried.

"It's going to be okay, baby. It will all be over soon." Serenity didn't know if her words were true, but she hoped they were. She prayed this would end without any bullets hitting anyone else she loved.

Lil Jugg ran through the kitchen entrance, gun up, spraying aimlessly. Vice took cover behind the half-wall and waited. One shot to the head. Jugg's body dropped with a thud onto the tile. Vice smiled, nodding his head, ready for war. He didn't know who these people were, but if they wanted a war, he was going to stand on the front line.

Kilo looked on in shock as his entire team dropped. He walked backwards out of the restaurant, still firing shots. Out front, he was still moving, creeping through the chaos like a ghost. He fired two more rounds at the glass, not caring who they hit. Valor charged through the smoke, but when he hit the sidewalk, Kilo was already peeling off, his SUV screeching into the street. Reason and Vice came out just a few seconds after, guns in hand, breathing hard.

"His ass got away, but I was able to get the license plate," Valor informed.

"You got their plate number? That's all we need to find out who the fuck that was," Karma spoke, running out of the restaurant. She pulled her phone from her purse and made a call. The moment it was answered, she told Valor to give her the plate number. The person on the other end told Karma that she would call her back in fifteen minutes.

Sirens howled from blocks away. Patrons from other tables huddled in corners. Blood stained the cream marble like permanent scars. Paramedics were already working on Shane, stabilizing him before taking him to the hospital. Serenity was in shock, but Reason stood near the busted entrance, eyes narrowed. Something in his gut told him the truth – that this was no random hit.

A few minutes later, Karma was walking back up to Reason with a name. "Yo, cousin, do you know somebody named Kenneth Williams?"

Reason's jaw clenched as he looked at the spent shells on the floor.

He turned, looking down at Karma. "Yeah, this nigga named Kilo that I thought was long gone."

Reason motioned for Serenity, and she walked over to him, still visibly shaken. Reason wrapped his arms around her before telling her to get the kids and get in the car. He told Shayla to follow them back to their parents' house. Kilo had started a war that Reason wasn't backing down from, but first, he had to ensure his family was safe. Valor and Vice got into the car with Shayla and Karma, and they all pulled off.

REASON STOOD on the front lawn of Serenity's parents' home, jaw tight, eyes scanning the dark corners of the block. Extra security cars lined the curb now – two on the street, one in the alley, and another parked across the neighbors' driveway. Armed men were also stationed at every possible entrance. Reason wasn't taking any chances with the safety of his family.

Valor stepped outside, gun on his hip. "You good?"

"Nah," Reason said, pacing the walkway. "But they will be." He nodded toward the house. "The kids. Her people. Ain't nobody gon' touch them. Not while I'm breathing. I ain't gon' be good until I body that nigga."

Valor leaned against the porch post, watching him closely. "Who was it?"

Reason stopped pacing and looked at his cousin. "This bitch ass nigga named Kilo."

Valor frowned. "Why the hell he come spraying on a wedding rehearsal?"

Reason sighed, rubbing a hand over his beard. "Couple years back, he robbed three of my spots. Thought he was slick. Me and Ace put a hit out on him, but the bullet missed. It hit his twin brother instead. Brick," Reason said. "I guess that nigga still want payback for that shit."

Valor nodded slowly, piecing it together. "Yeah, that's cool and all, but how that nigga know we was gonna be there? Who all knew about the rehearsal dinner?"

"Shit, didn't nobody know about the rehearsal other than a few people in my crew and the people that were at the rehearsal. Nobody there fucks with Kilo though."

"I hear you, but that nigga didn't just show up out the blue. Somebody had to tell him we were there. So, what we doing about this shit because we not letting this shit fly?"

"Let it fly? Nigga, I know you know me better than that. I'm not letting shit fly. That nigga gon' die. Then, I'ma marry my woman and live happily ever after."

Valor cracked his knuckles. "I'm down with whatever you down with."

<hr>

KILO STORMED through the door of his house, slamming it behind him. His face was twisted in rage, the veins in his neck pulsing. Sweat dripped from his brow, and blood was all over him. He couldn't believe three of his goons were dead, while Reason was still alive. They had failed their mission, and Kilo was pissed. He kicked over a chair and grabbed a bottle of Hennessy from the counter, drinking it straight from the bottle. Kilo drank half of it before smashing it against the wall.

"Fuck!" he roared.

He paced the living room like a caged animal, his jaws clenched, fists balled, and heart pounding. This wasn't the way it was supposed to go. They were supposed to spray and slide out. Kilo was supposed to be the one that came out on top. However, Reason had been more prepared than Kilo thought. Now, because of that, Roc, Tre-5, and Lil Jugg were all dead. He pulled his phone from his pocket and hit Chrome's contact in his phone.

"What up doe?" Chrome answered.

"It went left," Kilo growled. "They was ready, too ready. Shit went left, and it's all bad."

Chrome didn't respond right away. Instead, he let Kilo continue.

"I lost three of my niggas tonight," Kilo said, quieter now. "I thought we had that shit in the bag. But them muthafuckas he was with was blastin' back."

"Look, man, I ain't got no beef with Reason, but I'm down for whatever you want to do," Chrome spoke.

Kilo sat down on the couch, elbows on his knees, chest still rising and falling. "I'm not letting this go. Not after what he did to Brick. This ain't over at all."

Chrome stayed silent.

"I came loud," Kilo muttered, more to himself than to Chrome. "Next time, I'm coming smart."

Friday

Chapter Six

THE SUN WAS BARELY PEEKING out through the clouds when Reason, Valor, and Vice gathered in the den of Reason's house. It was five thirty in the morning, and the energy in the room was thick with everyone's trigger fingers itching. Reason paced in front of the large window. They'd just come back from a maybe mission. The address that was attached to his license wasn't his. Reason, Valor, and Vice had run up in the spot, guns held high, just to find out nobody lived there.

"I should've smoked that nigga when I had the chance," Reason muttered. "I let too much slide. Now, my family gotta pay for it."

Valor sat on the edge of the couch, one arm slung over the backrest, his other hand on the armrest. "So, what's the play, cousin? We sitting here waiting for another hit, or we moving first?"

Vice was in the corner, leaning against the wall, flipping a knife between his fingers. "We find that nigga, Kilo. Hunt him before he circles back. Cause he will. It's clear that he got a bone to pick with you, and that nigga ain't gon' stop until he gets yo ass. So, we gotta get him first. And it's clear he got a nigga working for him on the inside, so we gotta get that nigga too."

Reason stopped pacing and looked at both of them.

"I want eyes on the east and the west side. Kilo gotta be hidin' somewhere close. He ain't gon' run. Not until he feel like he got the last word."

"We need someone who knows his movements," Vice added. "We need to find that muthafucka he been talking to. We find him, we find Kilo."

Valor nodded his head, agreeing with his brother.

Reason narrowed his eyes. "I don't know who it would be. I got an entirely different crew when I got back into the game after my accident. Shit, the only person that's still around is Chrome."

"Then that's who the fuck it is. I don't know shit about Chrome or Kilo, but what I do know is that somebody told Kilo what restaurant we were going to be at. And if that's the only nigga that could have done it, then he did it," Valor chimed in.

Reason nodded his head slowly, not wanting to believe it. However, he knew that it couldn't have gone any other way. Chrome was the only person that knew both Kilo and where the rehearsal was being held. He shook his head at Chrome's betrayal, and he knew he would have to kill him.

"I'm not waiting for Kilo to make his next move. Everything gets handled today. I don't want Serenity worrying about shit tomorrow other than remembering her vows," Reason spoke, looking from Valor to Vice.

Vice pushed off the wall. "You already know we with you. We can ride out right now and go get that nigga, Chrome. I'm sure he the key to finding Kilo."

Valor stood, cracking his knuckles. "I'm for sure ready to go to war, but we need at least a few hours of sleep before we do anything else."

"Yeah, we can't do what we trying to do off no sleep. We all need to be alert. We can leave out later on today. For right now, everybody get some sleep."

They both nodded before walking to their rooms. They all knew what had to be done and were all ready for whatever.

SERENITY WOKE up to the low hum of a box fan in the window and the faint scent of coffee drifting up from downstairs. For a second, it almost felt like she was a teenager again, back in her old room with the faded lavender walls and the creaky wooden floor her daddy always meant to fix. Her chest tightened before her eyes even opened. The weight of what happened last night pressed down on her like a brick. The gunshots, the screams, the blood. It all played in her mind like one bad dream; however, it was reality. Her body tensed as the memory replayed in fragments. It had all happened so fast, but the aftermath stretched endlessly.

She sat up slowly, her muscles stiff from a restless night on the old twin mattress. Her silk bonnet had slipped halfway off, and her curls were frizzy around the edges, but she didn't even bother to fix it. For the first time since she'd been with Reason, she felt scared. It was not the surface-level nerves she expected to feel before her wedding day but the deep, soul-shaking kind of fear that made her question if they would even live long enough to make it to the altar.

Tears burned in the corners of her eyes, but she blinked them back. She had to be strong. She had two little people that were depending on her to be. Serenity swung her legs over the edge of the bed and stared at her hands. Her engagement ring was still there, glinting in the soft morning light, a symbol of a promise that Reason had made to her. She smiled.

Her phone buzzed on the nightstand, and her heart leaped. It was a text from Reason. She was praying that it was him telling her that he'd handled everything, and they were all in the clear.

Good morning, baby. I love you.

Serenity pressed the phone to her chest and closed her eyes. "I love you too," she whispered.

A soft knock at the door took Serenity away from her thoughts.

"Come in," she said, her voice low.

Her mother peeked in, already dressed, her gray streaks tucked neatly under a silk head wrap. "Hey, baby. You okay?"

Serenity nodded yes, even though it was a lie.

Stephanie stepped in, sitting beside her and rubbing her back gently.

"I didn't sleep," Serenity confessed. "Every time I closed my eyes, I heard the gunshots again."

"I know," Stephanie whispered. "It shook all of us. But baby, you're still here. We all still here, and that in itself is a blessing. That's what matters right now."

Serenity nodded slowly, but her lips trembled. "I don't want to walk down that aisle tomorrow with fear in my heart."

Stephanie looked into Serenity's eyes. "Then don't. Walk down it with love. Walk down it with strength. That man loves you enough to lay his life on the line, and you love him enough to start a new one with him. Don't let somebody else's evil steal what God gave you."

That broke the dam. Serenity leaned into her mother's shoulder and cried. She did love Reason, but would walking down the aisle tomorrow put the lives of her children at risk? That was something that Serenity refused to do. She wasn't saying that she didn't want to marry Reason because she did. However, she thought it might be best if they changed the location of the wedding.

"I just wanted this to be perfect," she said through tears.

Stephanie kissed her forehead. "It is perfect, baby. Not because everything went right but because you still got love. You still got family. And come tomorrow, you gon' have a husband who would move heaven and hell to protect you. I know in my heart that Reason is going to handle this. You see all the security he got outside the house right now? Shit, he will have a hundred times that at the wedding. That man would never put you and those children in harm's way."

Serenity sniffled and nodded. Her mother was right. Reason would do anything for her, and she knew it. She wiped her tears and looked up at Stephanie. "You right, Mama."

"I know. Mommy always knows best. Now go wash yourself up and come downstairs for breakfast."

About thirty minutes later, Serenity walked into the kitchen. Scotland and Easton were already at the table with their plates in front of them. Karma and Shayla were sitting at the kitchen island, and Serenity's father sat at the head of the kitchen table, scrolling through his phone. Serenity made her plate and sat between Scotland and Easton.

"You ready to get married tomorrow, cousin?" Karma asked, looking back at Serenity.

"Yeah, I'm ready to marry my man. Yesterday was..."

"Just that, yesterday, and we ain't gon' dwell on it. You gon' let them men handle it and leave it at that. Tonight, though, is yo bachelorette party, and we bout to turn up," Shayla chimed in, cutting Serenity off mid-sentence.

"Bachelorette party? How the hell we gon' do that with these kids in the house?" Serenity asked, looking over at Scotland and Easton.

"Girl, yo man got us a penthouse suite downtown for the night. I spoke to Reason this morning, and it sounds to me that he has everything under control. I've already called the dancers and told them about the change in location. We gon' get lit." Shayla laughed.

Serenity smiled as she shook her head. She couldn't believe how Reason had thought of every detail down to her bachelorette party. She couldn't believe she'd been so lucky to find a man as good as Reason. At that moment, all her doubts melted away, and somehow, she knew everything would be alright.

Chapter Seven

THE HOUSE WAS quiet when Reason opened his eyes. The sun was already high in the sky, casting golden streaks through the blinds in his bedroom. It had taken him forever to fall asleep, and even then, rest came in fragments. But now, he was awake with a clear mind. He rolled onto his back, staring at the ceiling for a long moment before sitting up. His body ached. It was not from physical pain but from the pressure of holding everything together.

He'd wanted the night to be about celebrating their love with family and friends. Instead, it turned into gunfire and fear. Reason threw on a black T-shirt and a pair of black joggers then padded down the stairs barefoot, expecting to find Valor and Vice still asleep in the guest rooms. However, Reason was surprised to see them already awake. Both their doors were opened and their beds already made.

He found them both in the kitchen. Valor was loading clips at the table, fingers flying with precision. Vice leaned against the fridge with a Glock tucked into his waistband.

"Did y'all sleep?" Reason asked.

Valor didn't look up. "Nah, not really. We been up. You?"

"Kinda tossed and turned." Reason exhaled.

Vice smirked. "Ain't nobody sleepin' right after a war cry like that. Not unless they dead."

Reason nodded, rubbing the tension from the back of his neck. "I was coming to wake y'all up, so we could move."

"You late," Valor said, locking in the last clip and standing up. "We been ready."

"Let's get it then."

They got dressed in silence. All black, gloves and bulletproof vests. Reason knew he was about to go reclaim his peace. Vice grabbed the duffle bag filled with extra clips, duct tape, and a burner phone just in case. Valor slung a shotgun over his shoulder and picked up one of the ski masks that were on the table. Reason slid a .40 caliber into his waistband and zipped his hoodie halfway. Once they were set, he looked them both in the eyes.

"No mistakes. No talking more than we need to. We in and out, but we make it clear this wedding gon' be protected at all costs. I don't give a fuck if that nigga hands us Kilo on a silver platter. We bodying both them niggas tonight."

Valor nodded. "You already know you talking our language."

Vice's eyes lit up with something that looked too close to joy. "Been waitin' to fuck these niggas up since yesterday."

They left the house without saying a word. The drive across town was short but tense. Reason gripped the wheel, jaw tight, music low. Chrome's house was off 7 Mile, tucked behind a row of houses with boarded-up windows and rusted fences. They pulled up slow, tires crunching gravel. A stray dog barked in the distance, making the soundtrack to their chaos. Reason parked in the alley behind the house. They stepped out, guns tucked but close, eyes sweeping every corner like sharks smelling blood. This was no friendly visit, and Chrome would soon know that.

They came in through the back door. Vice picked the lock and was able to get the door open within seconds. Reason stepped inside first, gun leading his way. They moved through the kitchen cautiously, silent and focused. Chrome was in the living room, kicked back on his couch, headphones on, game controller in hand. He was playing *2K* like he didn't have a damn worry in the world.

Vice reached him first, snatching the controller out his hands before cracking it against the wall. Chrome barely had time to jump up before Valor grabbed him by the throat and slammed him back onto the couch.

"What the fuck?!" Chrome choked, struggling.

Reason stepped forward. His gun hung low at his side, finger on the trigger.

"Keep yelling. I'll decorate this couch with your front teeth," Vice warned, pressing the muzzle of his pistol into Chrome's temple.

Chrome stilled, his eyes darting between the three of them. He knew if they were already in his house, he was as good as dead.

"You got sixty seconds to start talkin'," Reason spoke, voice flat. "And don't lie. Cause if I smell bullshit, I'ma let Vice take your jaw off."

Chrome swallowed. "Man, I don't even know what y'all on."

Valor backhanded him hard enough to draw blood. "Stop the bullshit, nigga. You know why we here."

Reason crouched low in front of him. "You the only nigga that wasn't at my rehearsal dinner that knew where it was. You wanna tell me how the fuck Kilo found out about it? That nigga came in firing bullets right where my children and wife were sitting. You better start talking and fast."

Chrome's lip trembled – not in fear but anger. He spat blood to the side and looked down at the gun pressed into his ribs.

"Aight," he muttered. "Aight, damn. I ain't want no part of it, but shit got messy."

Reason didn't blink. "What got messy?"

Chrome exhaled. "Ace. He set you up. All them lil' hits on your spots? That was him. He fed the idea that it would get me, Kilo, and Brick on top. The first spot we didn't know was yours. But when we found out, we didn't stop. Shit, the money was coming fast, but we was splitting it four ways. We didn't see at the time that we were all just pawns in his game. The truth was that nigga wanted you out the picture, so he could slide in on Kalahni."

Valor's jaw tensed. "Grimy ass nigga."

Reason didn't flinch, but his eyes went cold.

"And Kilo?"

Chrome looked like he wanted to crawl into the floorboards. "Kilo think you the one who dropped Brick."

Reason's stare sharpened. "That ain't the case. I put a hit out on Kilo when Ace brought back the information that he was the one hittin' my spots. Ace told me that he sent you to deal with Kilo, but you ended up getting his twin. I didn't know Brick or Ace had shit to do with the hits til now."

"Look, Reason, I don't have no beef with you. Truth is, I always looked at you as the big homie. You taught me a lot about the game. But Kilo is my cousin, so I gotta ride with my family."

The room froze. Valor and Vice both straightened up but still kept their weapons drawn.

Reason's voice dropped to a whisper. "Fuck you just say?"

"I'm Kilo and Brick's blood cousin," Chrome said slowly. "Our mamas were sisters. Before our mothers died, they taught us that family was everything and that we should always stick together. So, my loyalty will always be with them."

Reason stood. His entire body was tight with fury. "Where the fuck is Kilo?"

Chrome shook his head. "Even if I did know, I wouldn't tell y'all. It's family over everything. Y'all already got into my house, so I know how this shit ends. Y'all came here to kill me so just get that shit over with."

Vice cocked his gun. "Then it ain't no reason to keep questioning you." Vice fired one shot in Chrome's head, killing him instantly.

Reason turned for the door with Valor and Vice following. They left just as quiet as they came, rushing through the alley and into the car. They were just about to pull off when they noticed a car pull up into Chrome's driveway. They sat for a moment, waiting to see who would get out the car.

"Yo, that's Kilo." Reason pointed out.

They ducked low, guns drawn as they watched him walk up to the door. Reason's trigger finger itched as he looked at the man who wreaked havoc on his wedding weekend. He knew this would be his only time to get him, and it couldn't be sloppy.

"Don't move," he continued.

<hr>

KILO UNLOCKED the front door without knocking. He never knocked on Chrome's door. Not once in his life. However, today something felt off. The door creaked open slowly. When the smell of weed didn't immediately hit his nose, Kilo got nervous. He stepped in slowly, closing the door behind him.

"Chrome?" Kilo called out, stepping inside.

When Chrome didn't answer, he called out to him louder. That was when he saw Chrome's body. He was slumped on the couch, head tilted to the side, blood running from it. It was clear to Kilo that he was dead. Kilo didn't move for a long time. He just stood there, staring at his cousin like the sight of his body hadn't fully registered yet.

It was the way he was sitting that got to Kilo the most. It was almost like he died in fear. Like whoever came in there didn't just kill him. They cornered him unexpectedly. That realization set something off deep in Kilo's chest. It wasn't just anger; it was rage. He walked up to the body, crouched low, and looked Chrome dead in the face.

"Damn..." Kilo whispered.

He stood back up and looked around the house. The back door was still open, and he knew that was how they came in. Kilo's jaw clenched as it all came together. There was only one person who could have been behind this, and Kilo knew it was Reason. Kilo didn't cry or scream out in anger. It wasn't because he wasn't mad but because he knew he needed all the energy he had to kill Reason.

"I promise you that nigga gon' die. And when I kill him, you and Brick better fuck him up in the afterlife."

Kilo walked back out the front door, got in the car, and pulled off down the street. He wasn't going to rest until he killed Reason. Fuck hitting him at his wedding tomorrow. Kilo was ready to handle it tonight, stopping any chance of Reason meeting Serenity at the altar.

Chapter Eight

SERENITY SAT on the couch in her parents' living room, thinking about what she was going to wear to her bachelorette party. She didn't have any of the items she needed to get ready there. She wanted to go out and have fun. Hell, she needed it after the way the weekend had started out. However, she knew that if she couldn't put that shit on, then she wasn't going. She'd purchased new everything for the night just last week; however, everything was at her house.

A few moments later, there was a knock on the door. Slowly, Serenity stood to her feet and walked toward the door. Looking out the peephole, she saw that it was one of the guards Reason had posted outside the house. Opening the door, Serenity greeted the guard before he handed her a black garment bag along with two Saks Fifth bags. Her eyes widened as a huge smile spread across her face. Serenity immediately knew those were the items she'd purchased for the night.

Damn, my man really thought of everything, Serenity thought as she took the bags from the man's hands. She thanked him before closing the door and going upstairs to her old bedroom. She placed the bags on the dresser before hanging the garment bag in the closet. She heard the little footsteps running down the hallway, and she smiled as Scotland and Easton ran into the room. Serenity opened her arms, wrapping them around the children and hugging them tightly.

"Mommy, do I get to wear my dress tomorrow?" Scotland asked, smiling up at Serenity.

"You sure do, baby, and Easton, you get to put on your suit. We gonna take pictures and have lots of fun."

"Auntie Shayla said it's gonna be a party." Easton beamed.

"It is, a big one. We gonna eat good food, dance, eat cake, and it's even going to be candy and cookies there."

"Cake, candy, and cookies? Can I have some?" Easton smiled from ear to ear.

"As much as you want, big man."

"We bout to go in the backyard and have a water fight. Grandma found some water balloons and water guns in the basement. You wanna come?" Scotland asked, looking over at Serenity with wide eyes.

Serenity looked over at the mirror and looked at her hair then down at her two wide eyed babies awaiting her answer. She walked over to the bottom drawer of her old dresser and rummaged through items until she came across two swim caps. *Ain't no way I'm getting my hair wet just hours before my bachelorette party,* Serenity thought.

"Yeah, Mommy is coming out. Let me change my clothes and wrap my hair."

Serenity put on a pair of black yoga shorts with a matching black crop top. She walked inside the bathroom, grabbed two shower caps, and a rubber band before heading back to the room. She placed a band around her edges before brushing her hair into a ponytail and placing the first shower cap on. Making sure that all her hair was neatly tucked inside, she then put on the two swim caps before placing the final shower cap on and making her way to the backyard.

The smell of charcoal filled the air as smoke curled into the summer sky as Serenity's father stood at the grill. Frankie Beverly and Maze played from a speaker on the porch. The sun was high, the grass was freshly cut, and Serenity couldn't help but smile as she heard Easton laugh when he hit Scotland with a water balloon.

"Girl, where the hell you going with all that armor on yo head? You sure you just coming out here for a water fight with the kids 'cause it look like you greased up for a brawl with Nemo?" Her father laughed as he flipped the burgers on the grill.

Serenity rolled her eyes, laughing. "Don't be tryna do too much, Daddy. Cause who bout to get they hair wet?"

"You look like you 'bout to be unda da sea with the little mermaid."

Her mother burst out laughing from the patio table. "Leave her alone, Richard. That girl hair cost more than your whole 'fit."

"I'm just sayin'!" He grinned, wagging his tongs.

"Okay, Daddy," Serenity said through a laugh, tossing a water balloon straight at his chest.

SMACK! It exploded right on his apron.

"Oh, so that's what we doin'?" he said, wiping water off his shirt. "Aight. Y'all done woke up the beast now!"

Scotland and Easton screamed and took off running across the yard, water guns already in hand. Serenity darted behind a lawn chair as her dad grabbed two Super Soakers from under the grill like they were military weapons. "Operation Soak and Destroy!" he hollered. "This backyard ain't safe no more!"

"Mom, help!" Serenity yelled, dodging a stream of water as her dad turned into a man on a mission.

"I'm on dry duty, baby." Stephanie laughed, sipping lemonade like she wasn't about to get hit next.

Scotland squealed with joy as she launched a water balloon that hit Easton square in the back. "Got you!" she yelled.

"No fair!" Easton shouted, pumping his own water gun and turning it on her.

Serenity ducked low behind the tree, peeking out just in time to see her daddy creeping up like he was in Vietnam. He had camouflage shorts on, socks pulled up to his knees, a pair of black slides, and his grill tongs still in hand.

"I see you, soldier!" she yelled, grabbing a bucket from behind the lawn furniture.

"Don't do it, Nene," he warned, smiling.

Before he could say another word, she did it. The whole bucket soaked his front side, and he stood there, frozen for two seconds, like he'd just seen his whole life flash before him. Then, he slowly took off his slides and waved it in the air. "You finna get this daddy whoopin' like it's 1998!"

"Go head. I wasn't even born until 1999 anyway," Serenity shrieked, water gun in hand, running across the yard barefoot while the kids screamed and hollered like they were in a water park. Her hair stayed wrapped tightly, edges unbothered, lashes still intact. She was soaked everywhere else, but that wrap? Not a drop.

"I ain't raising no dry-haired kids!" her dad yelled as he squirted water toward Scotland and Easton, chasing them behind the shed.

Back on the porch, Serenity's mom was filming the whole thing with a smirk. "They gon' talk about this summer forever."

By the time the water war ended, they were all dripping and breathless, laying across beach towels in the sun like they were really on the beach. Her father went back to the grill, flipping burgers and humming to himself.

"You want cheese on yours, Easton?"

"Yes please!" he called out, wiping his face with his wet shirt.

Richard made plates for everybody, even the guards Reason had posted around the house. Men who'd been stone-faced all day cracked smiles as he handed them foil-wrapped burgers with grilled onions and pepper jack cheese. "Y'all protectin' my baby," he said, patting one of them on the shoulder. "Y'all eatin' too."

Serenity sat with her legs crossed on a lawn chair, sipping a cold bottle of water, still laughing as her dad danced with a spatula in his hand to Teena Marie now playing through the speakers. For a brief moment, everything felt normal and simple, like her man wasn't at war just a few miles away.

THE BATHROOM MIRROR WAS FOGGY, but Serenity didn't care. Her face glowed beneath the soft steam, her skin warm and dewy from the long shower. The tension that had gripped her chest all morning had finally loosened. It wasn't gone, not completely, but tonight wasn't about that. Tonight was about laughter, drinks, and having fun with her girls.

"Serenity, you done yet?" Karma banged on the door like they were back in high school again, sharing one bathroom and fighting over the hot comb.

"Almost!" Serenity called, smiling.

She stepped into the bedroom, wrapped in a satin robe, her curls pinned up with gold clips, face fresh, bare, and beautiful. The smell of hot flat irons and Fenty body butter filled the air. Shayla was sitting cross-legged on the bed, doing her lashes, while Karma danced in front of the mirror, lip-syncing to Tinashe's *2 On* like they were back in 2014.

"Y'all remember when we used to pretend we was goin' to the club just to get dressed up in your mama's basement?" Karma laughed, hitting a hip roll like she was auditioning for *106 & Park*.

Shayla snorted. "Girl, we used to spray on *Love Spell* like it was holy water."

Serenity laughed, thinking back on the memory. "Well, tonight, we grown for real. And I'm about to step out lookin' like somebody's rich wife. Periodt."

"Correction," Shayla said, standing up and fluffing her hair. "You are about to be *Reason Alexander's* rich wife. Like, girl, how does it feel to be marrying Detroit's most infamous thug turned family man?"

Serenity smirked, but her eyes softened. "Like I'm exactly where I'm supposed to be."

The music switched to The Weekend's *Often*, and Shayla squealed, grabbing a brush to use as a mic while she twerked in her thigh-high socks. They moved around each other with ease, laughing and teasing. Serenity sat down at the vanity and began doing her makeup – a soft glam look, golden lids, wispy lashes, nude gloss. She set it off with a dewy mist before reaching for her fragrance of the night, Parfums de Marly's Oriana.

"That smell like money," Karma complimented, walking past her and sniffing dramatically. "Wife money."

Serenity grinned. "It should smell like wife money. My rich ass husband bought it."

By the time they were dressed, the room had transformed. Shayla wore a sheer mesh jumpsuit with rhinestones, hugging every curve. Karma chose a deep red mini dress with slits up the side and gold accessories that popped against her melanin. And Serenity, she wore white, a silky, fitted mini dress that wrapped around her body like it was made for her alone with thin spaghetti straps and an open back. It was the kind of dress that made men stop talking mid-sentence and stare. The kind of dress that said, "I'm taken, *but* I'm still the one."

They all wore heels high enough to make ankles ache, but none of them cared. Tonight was about celebration. Escaping the weight of everything they couldn't control and stepping into the joy they still had the power to claim. Serenity checked herself in the full-length mirror one last time, loving what she saw.

"You ready?" Karma asked.

Serenity exhaled, feeling the bass of Megan Thee Stallion rumbling through the Bluetooth speaker now.

"Ready," she said, turning toward the door. She didn't know what the night would bring. But for this one moment, she was choosing joy.

Chapter Nine

R EASON WAS sure to keep a steady two-car distance behind Kilo's car. The sun was gone now, swallowed by nightfall. Streetlights flickered with an eerie orange glow that made everything feel like a warning. Reason sat behind the wheel, jaw tight, eyes laser-focused on the car ahead. There were no words spoken or music playing, just the low hum of tires rolling over cracked pavement. Vice sat in the front passenger seat, checking the grip on his chrome .45. Valor was in the back with a sawed-off shotgun across his lap and a grin on his face like he'd been waiting for this moment his whole damn life.

"I can't wait to get this nigga," Valor spoke, watching Kilo's car in front of them.

Kilo turned down a narrow residential street then parked in front of a two-story brick house. He rushed out the car, not seeing Reason parked at the corner. Reason watched as Kilo jogged up the walkway and into the house. Once Kilo was inside, Reason, Valor, and Vice all got out the car. They were ready, dark clothes, hoods up, gloves on. Reason carried a 9mm. Vice had a .45 and a long blade strapped to his hip. Valor cradled the sawed-off under his arm like it was an extra limb.

When they reached the backyard, Reason held up a fist, signaling them to freeze. A light flickered in one of the upstairs windows. Reason watched as Kilo poured brown liquor into a cup, drinking it down before pouring another.

"Time to end this shit," Valor muttered.

"Let's make it loud," Vice added, licking his teeth.

Reason shook his head. "Nah. Not loud, just personal."

A few moments later, upstairs, a bedroom light flickered, and that was when they entered the house, coming in from the back door just as they had done in Chrome's spot. They crept through the house quietly, being sure not to alert him of their presence. Valor kicked open the bedroom door, the sawed-off aimed straight at Kilo's chest.

Kilo spun around, eyes wide. "Yo, what the f…"

BOOM!

The blast hit him in the shoulder, slamming him into the wall. Blood sprayed across the curtains as he slid to the floor, coughing and clutching the wound.

"I *knew* it was you, Reason," Kilo hissed, grimacing through the pain. "You killed Chrome. Now, you here to kill me too, huh?"

Reason stepped in slowly, gun in hand. "Nah, Kilo. We ain't come for you." He crouched low, his voice calm. "You came for me. We just here finishing what you started"

Kilo laughed, blood dripping from his lips. "Finishing what I started? After all the dirt you done did, Reason? Nigga, if you wouldn't have killed Brick, none of this would be going on."

Reason leaned in. "I didn't kill Brick. That was all Ace. But you came for my family. At my fucking rehearsal dinner. With my kids and my woman standing right there. You let your grief turn into a grudge… and you forgot who I was."

Kilo tried to sit up, but Vice shoved him down with a boot to the chest, holding him there. "Sit yo ass the fuck down."

"Fuck all y'all," Kilo spat. "Y'all caught me slippin', cool. Y'all here to kill me so just get it over with."

Valor stepped forward and cracked the stock of the shotgun across Kilo's jaw. Blood and teeth hit the floor. Kilo groaned, eyes rolling back. Reason dropped down and grabbed Kilo by the collar, dragging him to his knees like a puppet.

"You should have never came for my family."

Vice pulled the blade from his hip, a long, curved knife with a jagged edge that gleamed like cold fire. He had one just like it at home, so when Reason showed it to him, Vice knew he had to use it. "You ain't bout to die fast, but you damn sure dying."

He sliced deep into Kilo's thigh, blood spurting like a faucet. Kilo screamed out in pain, causing Vice to chuckle. Valor stuffed a balled-up rag that was on the floor into Kilo's mouth and duct-taped it shut.

"I want you to feel *everything*," Reason whispered. "Just like I felt when I had to watch my woman and children hit the ground to avoid the bullets you were firing."

He put his gun down on the bed. This wasn't a shooting anymore; the bullet was much too good for Kilo. Valor and Vice held Kilo still as Reason wrapped a cord around his neck, slow and methodical – not to kill, just to choke. Just enough to take his breath away. Then, they took turns. Valor broke fingers. Vice cut tendons. Reason beat him with fists and elbows until Kilo's face no longer looked human.

Finally, Reason knelt down beside him, breathing heavily. His shirt soaked in blood. His knuckles raw. "You should've left us alone."

Kilo's eyes fluttered, unfocused. His body slumped. Reason stood to his feet, grabbing his gun from Kilo's bed. He placed the barrel to Kilo's forehead before firing a single shot. Kilo dropped flat, blood pooling from his head. They wrapped the body in a rug they found in the living room. They carried Kilo's body out the back door and back to the car. They placed Kilo into the trunk before getting inside the car and pulling off.

Vice lit a cigarette and cracked the window with Valor lighting one as well. Reason didn't say a word, just kept his eyes on the road as he drove in silence. When they reached the river, they didn't hesitate before throwing the body inside. The streets were down one less bitch ass nigga with Kilo gone.

***

SERENITY STOOD in front of the floor-to-ceiling windows, sipping champagne from a crystal flute, her brown skin glowing under the suite's golden light. Her long curls cascaded down her back. She smiled as she watched her girls dancing around the suite, hyped off tequila and The City Girls. Reason had spared no expense when he booked the suite for her last night out as a single woman. The view was ridiculous, the liquor was top shelf, and the energy was a vibe.

"Okay, bitch, it's time!" Shayla cheered, walking up to Serenity with her cup held high.

"Time for what?" Serenity asked, raising a brow, already tipsy.

Shayla grinned, biting her bottom lip. "Time for the real show."

Before Serenity could say another word, the lights in the suite dropped low, and GloRilla's *Yeah Glo!* thumped through the surround sound speakers. The door opened and in walked three men dressed like they'd stepped straight out of a fantasy. One wore a fireman outfit. He was tall, about six foot four, with chocolate brown skin and huge muscles. Another was shirtless in slacks with suspenders. He was light-skinned with a low haircut. He was just as tall as the other man but much skinnier. The third man had on a Detroit police uniform that hugged his body like a second skin. He was a couple inches shorter than the other men, but his sexy face and even sexier muscles made up for it. Shayla and Karma screamed as Serenity stood there in shock.

"Damn! Are y'all serious? I didn't know y'all were getting three," Serenity whispered, her mouth wide open.

"Oh, but we did," Karma yelled, fanning herself and already pulling singles out of her custom "Bride Tribe" clutch.

Serenity clutched her chest, laughing. "Y'all are outta pocket for this! These niggas look like y'all found them on the gram."

"That's because we did." Shayla laughed.

The men spread out like they had done this hundreds of times before, and they had. The music changed to Chris Brown's *Take You Down*, and the fireman was on Serenity before she could finish her drink. He lifted Serenity gently into his arms, spinning her in the air like she weighed nothing. He laid her in the oversized velvet armchair like a queen being presented her throne. He danced slow, sensual, commanding her undivided attention. His abs flexed as he moved, his eyes locked onto hers like she was the only one in the room.

"Oh, my God," Serenity whispered, blushing hard.

Behind her, the girls were hollering, throwing money like they were in Magic City. Champagne spilled across the table when Shayla knocked the bottle over, but no one cared. Karma was throwing money like it was going out of style as the man danced. Serenity couldn't believe this was happening. She knew that her sister and cousin wanted to have fun tonight, but she didn't think the male dancers would be like this.

The officer danced next, his uniform shirt unbuttoned halfway down. He pulled a pair of cuffs from his belt and handed them to Serenity with a smirk.

"What you want me to do with these?" she asked, already giggling.

He bent low, voice deep and playful. "Whatever you want, Mrs. Alexander."

"Ooooh!" Shayla screamed.

The last dancer, the one in suspenders, slid onto the floor in front of her, rolling his body.

"This man gotta be a sin," Serenity muttered, covering her eyes. "I can't do this. I'm getting married tomorrow!"

"Exactly why you can," Karma shouted. "Let loose, baby!"

The dancers rotated between girls, but they kept coming back to Serenity, knowing it was her night. By the time *WAP* blasted through the speakers, all three men were down to their thongs. The ladies had kicked their heels off, and shots were lined up on the marble island in the kitchen. Serenity's legs were sore from dancing, and her abs hurt from laughing. Serenity was enjoying herself and was happy she was able to have this night out.

As the dancers exited, still dripping in sweat, they each kissed Serenity's hand and congratulated her. The suite settled down into post-party haze. The music stayed low, and the AC was blasting. Serenity collapsed onto the plush white couch, cheeks flushed, chest still rising and falling from dancing so hard.

"That was insane," she breathed. "I don't even know what just happened."

"You just had the hottest bachelorette party in Detroit, sis." Shayla smiled, refilling her glass.

Karma flopped down beside her and passed her a lemon drop shot. "Toast time." She smiled, holding up her glass. "To Serenity, the woman who showed us that true love does exist. Who didn't just find a good man but helped heal one. You deserve this. You deserve him. And most of all, you deserve to feel like the goddess you are every damn day."

"Amen," Shayla added, clinking her glass.

Serenity swallowed hard, eyes misting. "Y'all trying to make me ugly cry."

"Let it out, baby," Karma spoke. "This your moment."

Serenity stood up slowly, still holding her shot.

"To my sista and cousin, thank you." She smiled, looking around at the two women who'd seen her through everything from baby-daddy drama and the heartbreak of his passing to her taking a chance and finding love again. "Thank you for being my tribe. For seeing me. For lifting me up when I forgot who I was. I love y'all down."

Tears fell freely now, and nobody tried to stop them. She downed her shot and set the glass down gently, a full smile stretching across her face.

"We love you too," Karma replied, wrapping her in a hug.

"You know we love you, sis," Shayla spoke, joining in on the hug.

They sat on the couch, having one more drink, as they talked about tomorrow's events. When they were done, they all went to their rooms. Serenity's phone rang, and she looked at it, seeing it was Reason.

"Are you ready to become Mrs. Alexander tomorrow?" he asked the moment she answered the phone.

"I can't wait to meet you at that altar, baby."

"I took care of that little problem we had. Everything is going to be perfect tomorrow. I just wanted to tell you that I love you, and I can't wait to become your husband tomorrow."

Serenity smiled. "I love you too. And I can't wait to become your wife."

That night, Serenity slept peacefully, knowing her man had everything handled.

Saturday

Chapter Ten

Sunlight spilled through the wall of windows like golden silk, casting long beams across the soft comforter in the penthouse suite. Serenity lay still for a moment, wrapped in white linen. Her eyes opened slowly, lashes brushing against the pillowcase as her lips parted in a breath that felt brand new. It was her wedding day. It was not in a dream or fantasy but in real life and with real love to a man who had chosen her, protected her, and stood by her through pain, trauma, and healing.

Tears welled up in her eyes instantly. It was not the kind born from stress or nerves but the kind that came when you looked at your life and realized that God really didn't forget about you. She sat up slowly, curling her legs beneath her, and bowed her head right there in the center of the king-sized bed.

"God," she whispered, her voice already thick with emotion, "thank you." She closed her eyes, hands pressed together in her lap. "Thank you for bringing me through everything I thought would break me. Thank you for keeping me even when I didn't want to be kept. Thank you for watching over Easton, Scotland, and Reason. And for giving me a man who sees me, loves me, and protects me the way You do. God, I've prayed for a day like this, and I never thought I'd live to see it. Thank you for proving me wrong." Her breath caught.

"I give today to you, Lord. Every minute of it. Every step, smile, and tear. Let it be full of joy and covered in peace. And please... please let Reason feel Your presence too. Let him know he's safe. That he made it. That love can still win. And that Peaches will be with him every step of the way."

She paused, lips trembling.

"And God, thank you for loving me when I didn't know how to love myself. I promise I won't ever take that for granted again."

A soft knock at the door pulled her back to Earth. She wiped her face, already smiling.

"Come in!"

Shayla peeked her head in. "You up, Bridezilla?"

Serenity laughed. "Girl, you know damn well I ain't no bridezilla."

Shayla stepped in, eyes twinkling, with Karma right behind her, holding two iced coffees. "Rise and slay, baby girl. It's the big day!"

Serenity climbed out of bed with a full body stretch and walked toward them with open arms. The three women hugged, giggling, their excitement vibrating through the room like music.

"Today is the day you become Mrs. Alexander. You ready, sis?" Shayla beamed.

"I'm more than ready. I can't wait to marry that man." Serenity smiled before making her way to the bathroom to take a shower.

Serenity allowed the water to run down her body as if it was cleansing who she used to be. Gone was the girl who cried herself to sleep just three summers ago. Gone was the woman who questioned if she was worthy of true love. Every insecurity she had had been washed away by Reason's love. She stepped out, glowing. She wrapped herself in a plush white robe before walking out of the bathroom.

Shayla handed her a small white bag. "This your 'something new' from me and Karma."

Serenity opened it slowly, finding a delicate diamond anklet. "Damn, y'all tryna make me cry already. I love it. It's beautiful. Thank y'all so much."

"You're welcome. We just glad you like it." Karma smiled.

They gathered their things, making sure they didn't leave anything behind. As they stepped onto the private elevator that would take them down to the driver waiting out front to take them to the venue, Serenity turned one last time and looked at the suite. It was her last morning as a fiancée, her last hours as *just* Serenity. When she walked through the doors of her home tonight, she would walk through as Mrs. Alexander.

Serenity, Shayla, and Karma arrived at the venue about twenty minutes later. Brielle and Nyla met them there, ready for the lovely day they all knew it would be. The elevator doors opened to the top floor of the venue, and for a moment, Serenity stood still, taking it all in. Before her was the bridal suite, and it was breathtaking. The entire space had been transformed to fit Serenity.

The walls were a soft blush velvet with gold trim that glimmered every time the light shifted. Floor-to-ceiling windows let sunlight pour in, casting diamonds across the white marble floors. A vintage-style vanity lined one wall with matching gold-framed mirrors, while plush ivory chairs and blush-pink chaise lounges were scattered throughout the room. In the center, a chandelier of floating crystal drops sparkled like frozen rain, and directly beneath it, a round table sat with chilled Rosé, sparkling water, and elegant trays of finger foods.

There were white roses and peonies in pink-tinted vases, lavender eucalyptus bundles tucked into corners, and a huge gold-framed floor mirror near the dressing area that read, "Today She Becomes His Forever."

Serenity stepped inside and whispered, "This is crazy."

Shayla grinned. "It's all for you. Today is your day."

Karma nodded. "Yeah, this your type of vibe. Soft but bossy."

Before Serenity could say another word, the door opened and in walked Stephanie, smiling wide, with a sleepy-eyed but smiling Scotland holding her hand.

"There's my flower girl!" Serenity squealed, dropping to her knees.

Scotland ran into her arms, wrapping her tiny fingers into her momma's robe. "Mommy, you are about to look like a princess in your dress."

Serenity pulled her in tight, breathing her in. "And you look like my heart."

While Shayla helped Stephanie get Scotland settled with her snacks, Anita Baker's *Sweet Love* floated through the suite from the Bluetooth speaker on the windowsill. Miguel's *Adorn* came on right after. The nail techs arrived with rolling carts, ready to cater to the ladies. Serenity told her nail tech to start on Scotland first, painting her nails and toes a pretty peach.

Serenity went next. She chose an elegant medium coffin shape for her nails. They were painted in a milky white base with delicate gold foil marbling through the tips. Tiny peach and taupe stones, matching her wedding colors, accented her ring and pointer fingers. On her thumbs were hand-painted white roses, outlined in champagne shimmer, and a single small "R" in gold cursive was on the left pinky.

Karma and Shayla both opted for glossy rose-nude nails with gold chrome tips, while Brielle and Nyla went with taupe tips with ivory flowers. Stephanie went for a simple almond shaped set with a white French tip. Next came the hair stylists, rolling in carts with everything they needed to make the bridal party beautiful. The bridesmaids all got the same style, a half up half down style filled with flowing curls.

Scotland's hair was placed into two high buns with laid baby hairs that swirled like tiny waves along her forehead. The buns were full and fluffy, each wrapped with peach satin ribbon tied into little bows at the base. Scattered throughout the buns were tiny pearl pins that added a little extra to the style. Stephanie had her natural hair styled in huge curls that fell to her shoulders.

Serenity sat at the vanity, silent and still, as her stylist worked her magic. Her natural hair had been blown out and braided back. A dark brown lace front was placed on her head then glued down, lace binding in with her skin perfectly. It was then swooped into a sleek low bun, baby hairs were laid to perfection, and a delicate gold vine comb studded with pearls was tucked into the side. Loose tendrils curled softly around her nape and jaw, making the look timeless.

When the stylist finished and turned her toward the mirror, Serenity smiled, loving the finished look. The makeup artist walked up and started on Serenity's face. She started with a taupe smoky eye before applying her foundation. Once the contour and highlights were done, she lined Serenity's lips before painting them a soft nude. When she was finished, the makeup artist sprayed Serenity's face with matte setting spray. She told Serenity to close her eyes before turning her toward the mirror.

"You're all done, beautiful," the artist whispered.

Serenity opened her eyes, blinked once, and smiled at her reflection. She looked like a bride. But more than that, she looked like Reason's bride. A soft knock interrupted the moment.

Karma turned toward the door. "Who is it?"

A voice answered, low and smooth. "Vice."

The room tensed slightly, but Serenity smiled. "It's okay. Let him in."

Vice stepped inside, dressed in a taupe-colored tailored suit, chain tucked into his shirt. He wasn't smiling, but his eyes held a softness that hadn't been there since he touched down in Detroit. In his hands was a small white box with a gold ribbon and a folded envelope tucked beneath the bow.

He looked directly at Serenity. "This from Reason."

She stood slowly, heart already thudding against her chest as she took the gift with both hands.

Vice nodded once. "He said read the note first." Then, he turned and left, closing the door behind him without another word.

Serenity sat back down, the room completely silent now. Everyone's eyes were on her. She slid the envelope out gently and opened it. She recognized Reason's handwriting instantly, bold but careful, each letter shaped like it meant something. She read it softly to herself...

My Love,

I never knew peace before you. I knew survival. I knew war. I knew silence. But peace? Nah, I didn't know that until I watched you sleep beside me and realized I didn't have to be on guard anymore. That I didn't have to fight the world just to breathe.

You came into my life like sunlight through bullet holes. Soft but strong, flooding every crack I tried to seal shut. You saw every scar I tried to hide, and instead of running, you held me through the pain. You didn't just love me; you healed me.

I was drowning in my past when you found me. And somehow, without even trying, you taught me how to swim. How to rest and how to feel. You brought me back to life, Serenity. I'm not the same man I was before you, and I never want to be.

Today, I get to marry my miracle. I'll be waiting at the end of

*that aisle. And no matter what happens after today, just know I
found everything I ever prayed for in you.*
   Forever yours,
   Reason

Serenity's hands trembled as she folded the letter back into the envelope, pressing it gently to her chest. Her eyes burned, tears lining her lashes but never falling. Her makeup artist stood nearby, frozen, whispering, "Don't cry. Not yet."

Serenity exhaled, a soft laugh escaping through her tears.

Then, Karma whispered, "Girl, open the box."

With care, Serenity untied the gold ribbon and lifted the lid. Inside sat a velvet-lined jewelry case. She opened it and gasped. Inside was a custom diamond bracelet with three small charms hanging from it – a letter S for Serenity, a heart shaped lock and key, and an engraved dog tag that read, "His Peace". It wasn't just jewelry. It was their love story wrapped around her wrist.

Shayla covered her mouth. Karma wiped her eyes. Even the nail tech, still cleaning up her station, whispered, "That's the realest shit I ever saw."

Serenity slid the bracelet on, fingers trembling. It sparkled against her skin like it had always belonged there. She stood up slowly, holding the letter in her hand while the bracelet gleamed from her wrist. Then, she looked in the mirror, smiling.

"Okay," she whispered, voice full and steady. "Let's get dressed."

THE ROOM SMELLED like Tom Ford cologne and fresh cigars. Reason stood in front of the floor-length mirror, adjusting the cuff of his cream double-breasted suit jacket, custom-tailored to hug his broad chest and cinch just right at the waist. The silk lapels caught the light every time he moved. Underneath, his crisp white shirt was open just enough to show his diamond chain, the same one he wore the day he told Serenity "I love you" for the first time.

His slacks were perfectly pressed, tapering down to polished brown leather loafers. A diamond faced timepiece hugged his wrist, ticking calmly like his heart finally had rhythm. He looked like a king ready to marry his queen.

"Damn, bruh," Vice said from the leather couch, pouring up shots of D'usse. "You look like you got a billion in your bank account."

Reason smirked. "That's cause I damn near do."

The room erupted in laughter. The groomsmen, Valor, Vice, Reek, and Shane, all stood around in matching taupe suits. Shane's arm was in a sling from the bullet he'd taken at the rehearsal dinner, but he wasn't going to let that stop him. He told Reason that he didn't care if he had to be wheeled down the aisle. Nothing was going to stop him from being in his best friend's wedding, and Reason respected that. Despite everything – the hits, the drama, and the danger – they were still here, alive and breathing. And Reason was about to marry the woman who made surviving feel like living.

"To this nigga finding the love of his life," Valor said, raising his glass.

They all clinked their glasses and threw the liquor back. That was when a knock landed at the door.

"Who is it?" Reason asked, wiping his mouth.

"It's Shayla," she spoke. "I got somethin' for you."

Vice opened the door, and Shayla stepped in, radiant in her peach satin gown. She handed Reason a small white box with a letter attached and smiled softly. "From your bride."

The room quieted. Reason sat on the edge of the leather armchair, fingers slightly trembling as he opened the envelope.

My King,

I've seen you angry. I've seen you grieving. I've seen you guarded, and I've seen you broken. But even in your darkest moments, I never once doubted your heart. You walked through fire for me. You gave me safety when I didn't know what that felt like. You gave me space to heal without ever asking me to shrink.

You never had to tell me you loved me. I felt it in the way you came in and changed my life. I felt it in the way you protected my daughter like she was yours before I ever asked you to. And I felt it in every quiet night we spent in bed with no words. Just your arms around me, reminding me that I was finally home.

I don't care about the scars you carry. I don't care about the chapters you try to forget. I see all of you, Reason. And I still choose you. Today. Tomorrow. Forever. You've been my warrior. Now, let me be your peace.

I love you,
Serenity

Reason pressed the letter to his chest, jaw locked as he stared at the ground, trying not to let his groomsmen see the tears in his eyes. Reason took a deep breath, letting the weight of those words settle inside his soul like armor. Then, he opened the box. Inside, nestled in black velvet, was a solid gold Cuban link bracelet. It was engraved on the inside with the words, "Your Peace. Your Home. Your Forever."

Next to it was a vintage key on a delicate chain. Attached to the key was a tiny tag that read, "This is the key to the heart you healed."

He stared at it for a long time, holding it in his hands. No Rolex, no car, or stacks of cash could have moved him like this. This was a love that saw every inch of him, and he was happy he'd finally found it.

"I'm ready," he said finally, standing tall.

And he was. Not just to walk down the aisle but to step into a future that he knew he'd earned. He slipped the bracelet on, tucked the key into the inside pocket of his jacket, and looked in the mirror one last time.

"I'm comin', baby," he whispered to himself.

Chapter Eleven

THE GUESTS BEGAN to take their seats as *All My Life* by K-Ci & JoJo played gently through the speakers, filling the air with love. The ceremony space was nothing short of breathtaking. Draped from floor to ceiling were sheer panels in taupe and cream, softly backlit to cast a golden glow. Peach-toned florals spilled from crystal vases on every row, and floating candles flickered inside glass cylinders that lined the pathway from the back doors to the altar.

The chairs were arranged in perfect rows, each tied with a taupe-colored satin sash, and the scent of fresh roses, peach blossoms, and soft vanilla floated in the air like perfume. At the front of the room, the altar was framed with a circular arch wrapped in cream hydrangeas, peach roses, and vines of eucalyptus. Behind it was a shimmering curtain of lights that gave the illusion of stars, like Heaven had opened just for this moment.

But what drew every eye, especially Reason's, was the large portrait at the front of the ceremony space. Resting on an elegant easel trimmed in gold was a photo of Peaches. Serenity had chosen a photo of her laughing, head tilted back, smiling wide. The frame was surrounded by a cascade of peach and cream roses, and above it, a sign read, "Forever in our hearts. Forever a part of us."

Reason walked into the space, smiling at the picture. Rotimi's *I Do* played as Reason walked himself down the aisle and headed to the altar. Reason looked at the picture of Peaches once more when he got to the altar, nodding his head with a smile. "You made it, Mama."

The music shifted, and Anita Baker's *Sweet Love* played. The doors opened, and Stephanie began walking in, dressed in a peach two-piece skirt and blazer that was tailored to perfection. As she passed the guests, a few sniffled, others placed hands over their hearts. She walked slowly, every step filled with grace, until she reached the front row before taking her seat.

The music shifted again. Eric Benet and Tamia's *Spend My Life With You* began to play as Shane and Nyla walked in arm and arm down the aisle. Reek and Brielle walked out next, followed by Valor and Karma. When Vice and Shayla walked in, Reason knew that he was close to seeing Serenity. Behind them came Easton, looking like a little prince in a mini cream tuxedo with a peach bowtie. He held a sign that read, "Daddy, here comes Mommy."

The crowd let out soft awws, but the emotional swell truly came when Scotland followed close behind, carefully dropping petals from a white satin basket lined in peach lace. Her high puffball buns bounced with every step, the tiny pearls catching light as she focused hard on her job. Her dress was a miniature ball gown with a layered peach tulle skirt and a satin bodice.

Then, the music fell still before the first word of Yebba's *Heartbreak* echoed through the speakers. The entire room stood as the double doors opened. Serenity stepped forward slowly, her arm looped through her father's. Her dress was pure enchantment, a custom off the shoulder couture gown made of delicate ivory silk and nude mesh. The sweetheart neckline was overlaid with hand-embroidered lace that shimmered subtly with every step. The bodice hugged her perfectly before flaring out into a soft mermaid silhouette, the train long and regal, lined with tiny pearls and glass beads.

Her veil flowed from a pearl comb tucked into her romantic low bun, trailing behind her. The fragrance she chose was Maison Francis Kuurkdjian's Oud Satin Mood, allowing her to smell just as expensive as she looked.

Reason stood there, frozen, unable to move. His chest rose and fell, slow and deep, as his eyes welled up. He had seen her bare. He had seen her broken. But he had *never* seen her like this. She didn't just look like a bride. She looked like the beginning of everything he ever needed. He exhaled, lips trembling slightly, then closed his eyes for a brief second as if to memorize this moment forever.

As she reached the altar, the music faded. The officiating pastor, an older Black man with a slightly wrinkled face and low-cut, salt and pepper hair, stepped forward with a smile. He looked at Reason then Serenity and began speaking into the mic.

"Today, we stand in the presence of love itself. Not just the love between a man and a woman but the love of two people who allowed God to decide. We are all here to witness the union of Reason Alexander and Serenity Jones, whose journey to love might not have been easy. Hearts might have been broken, and tears might have been shed. But every wrong turn down the path to love led the two of you directly to each other, letting us all know that in the end, love will always win."

The room was silent as teary-eyed guests looked up at the happy couple.

The pastor turned to Serenity. "You may now share your vows."

She took a soft breath, her voice delicate but steady, as she took the mic from him and began.

"Reason, from the moment you came into my life, I've been learning what love truly means. I didn't understand peace until I heard your voice late at night, telling me I was safe. I didn't know protection until you stood between me and the world, offering up yourself so that I could feel safe."

She looked up at Reason, tears in her eyes as she continued.

"You never asked me to be perfect. You just asked me to be *me*. And because of that, I found my strength. I found my power, and I found my forever. You've seen every scar and kissed it. You never turned your back on me. Instead, you covered me and chose me."

She paused, blinking through tears.

"So today, I vow to do the same. I vow to honor your soul even when your spirit is tired. I vow to protect your heart like it's mine. I vow to speak life over your name, to pray over your peace, and to hold your hand through every season. I will never ask you to hide your pain. I will never fear your vulnerability. And I will never stop fighting for us."

She reached forward and touched his hand.

"Reason Alexander, I don't just love you. I *see* you. And I vow to never unsee you. Our love is one for the books. So, today, we make history."

When Serenity saw the tear slide down Reason's cheek, she stepped close, leaning up to kiss the tear away before mouthing the words, "I love you." The pastor gave a gentle nod, signaling it was Reason's turn.

He looked at Serenity, and for a moment, he couldn't speak. His throat tightened, and his jaw clenched. His fingers curled slightly, steadying himself from the flood of emotion rising in his chest. But Serenity, she just smiled, looking up at Reason. He reached into his pocket and pulled out a folded slip of paper, but he didn't open it. He kept his eyes on her, opening his mouth to speak.

"I never planned on being saved. I didn't think I deserved it. I've lived in places where love was a weakness, and silence kept you breathing. So, when I met you, Serenity, I didn't just fall for you. I *surrendered.* You didn't just walk into my life. God placed you here. You touched parts of me I thought were dead and were never coming back. You showed me that love cannot only heal the heart, but it can heal the mind, body, and soul.

"You gave me your heart with no conditions. You loved my son like he was born from your body. You embraced my pain like it was yours. You showed me that softness wasn't weakness. That peace wasn't boring and that forever with a woman that I truly love is possible."

He paused, his voice thickening.

"So, this is my vow to you. I will love you like it's my job every day with no days off. I will choose you first. I'll guard your heart like it's the last good thing left on this earth. I'll protect your smile even if it means bleeding for it. I promise to hold you when you're tired, to listen when you're quiet, and to fight with you when the world gets loud. I promise to pray for you, to grow with you, and to stay faithful not just to your body but to your soul. You are my safe place. My answered prayer. My second chance at life."

He reached into his jacket and pulled out the tiny vintage key she'd gifted him earlier.

"You gave me this key, but what you don't know is that you already unlocked everything in me the day you said you would be my wife."

He slipped the key into her hand and closed her fingers around it.

"So, this is yours again. Because I don't need to hold onto the key when I've already been set free."

The crowd was in awe. You could hear the sniffles as the guests wiped tear filled eyes. Even Valor and Vice stood there with their heads down, trying to hide their emotions. Reason took Serenity's hand, lifted it slowly, and kissed the back of it without looking away from her eyes. Then, he whispered the final part, just for her.

"I didn't know what love was until you came into my life. And I swear on everything I will never stop making *you* feel the same."

The pastor smiled at Reason and Serenity's vows before turning his attention to Easton and Scotland, who were now sitting in the front row next to Stephanie and Richard.

"This union isn't just about two hearts becoming one. It's about the beautiful *family* that is being created today. Easton and Scotland, would you both come join us up front?"

The guests murmured soft *awws,* and smiles bloomed across faces as the two little ones stood and walked up hand in hand, their tiny formal shoes tapping softly against the floor. Serenity knelt down to Scotland, while Reason did the same for Easton. From behind them, Karma stepped forward with a small white satin box and handed it to Reason. Inside were two delicate gold chains, custom made.

Easton's chain had a miniature lion's face with the letter S for Serenity, symbolizing her protection and love over his life forever. Scotland's chain had a tiny heart with the letter R in the middle, showing her that she would always have a father that would never leave her side. Serenity gently fastened Easton's around his neck, kissing the top of his head.

Reason carefully clipped Scotland's around her small frame and whispered, "I got you forever, baby girl."

Then, the pastor looked at the children. "Do you both accept the love of this family as your own?"

Easton grinned. "Yeah."

Scotland nodded shyly. "Yes."

The room *erupted* into gentle laughter and teary eyes. The pastor smiled, giving a slight nod.

"Now, Reason and Serenity will exchange rings, a symbol of their unending love and eternal bond."

Vice stepped forward, holding a small velvet box with his strong hands. Across the aisle, Shayla did the same, walking forward with her matching box for Serenity. They opened them in sync, revealing two perfect bands. They were custom-made, just like the love they represented.

Serenity reached for Reason's ring first. She took a slow breath and slid the matte platinum band onto his finger. The cool metal glided over his dark skin like it belonged there. The subtle taupe enamel inlay shimmered under the lights, and the hidden black diamond caught just enough glow to remind everyone that darkness could be turned into beauty.

"With this ring," she spoke softly, locking eyes with him, "I give you my soul and my loyalty. Forever."

Reason didn't look away. He nodded once, slow and full of reverence, before reaching for her ring. It sparkled just like her – delicate but strong. He held her hand gently, cradling it like it was the most sacred thing on Earth, and slid the oval-cut diamond ring onto her finger. The thin platinum band glittered with pavé diamonds, and the hidden halo gave it a soft glow from every angle.

"With this ring," Reason spoke, his voice thick but steady, "I give you everything I am. My protection, my name, and my legacy."

As the ring found its home, her hand trembled slightly. He rubbed her hand gently as he looked into her eyes. In that moment, with rings exchanged, children smiling behind them, and every scar they carried now transformed into a love that neither of them expected to have, they were pronounced husband and wife.

Without hesitation, Reason pulled Serenity close, kissing her passionately as the crowd cheered. Music began playing through the speakers again, Major's *This Is Why I love you*. Cameras flashed and guests stood to their feet. Reason and Serenity walked down the aisle for the first time as husband and wife as they walked through the double doors.

<hr>

AFTER THE CEREMONY, guests made their way to a nearby ballroom inside the venue, not expecting the beauty before them. The room was cast in a golden glow with taupe velvet drapery, peach lighting, and cream rose arrangements suspended from crystal chandeliers. Long rectangular tables were draped in silk linens and set with gold-rimmed plates, custom "Reason & Serenity" menus, and tall crystal glasses that sparkled like diamonds under the light. A massive, custom, LED dance floor sat in the center, glowing with soft peach light. Over it hung a floral chandelier with thousands of fresh roses and orchids dripping from the ceiling like a floating garden.

Each table had place cards with handwritten calligraphy. The head table, long, royal, and overflowing with candles, faced the dance floor and was elevated slightly, giving Reason and Serenity a perfect view of their party. Then, the lights dipped low. The DJ cued the mic.

"Ladies and gentleman, make some noise for the wedding party!"

The crowd clapped and hollered as the double doors opened, and the couples prepared to make their entrance, each with their own anthem. Shane and Nyla were the first to be introduced, coming in to Nipsey Hussle's *Racks in the Middle*. They did a sight two step before walking to their table. Next up was Reek and Brielle, who came in to Pardison Fontaine and Cardi B's Backin' It Up. Reek strutted in like he owned the block, spinning Brielle around before she popped her hip and winked at the camera.

Karma and Valor were next up, walking in to *No Flockin'* by Kodak Black. Valor slid in with one arm tucked in his suit. Karma popped her tongue and dropped low on beat. The crowd cheered them on. Next came Shayla and Vice, who came in to Drake and 21 Savage's *Knife Talk*. Vice walked in cool as ice, black shades on, calm like nothing fazed him. Shayla, looking fine as hell, matched his energy with a confident strut and a smirk that said, *"We ain't the ones."* They didn't do too much because they didn't have to.

Then, the music dropped completely. The DJ's voice came back through the mic with bass behind it. "Now, everybody stand up, turn your phones on, and make the loudest noise of the night for the couple of the decade! The reason we all came here! Mr. and Mrs. Reason Alexander!!" The room went *wild*.

The opening bassline hit, and the crowd erupted. Kid Ink and Chris Brown's *Show Me* played as the double doors opened. Reason and Serenity stepped through hand and hand. Reason had changed into a fresh cream tux with a peach satin lining. Serenity had changed too, now in a sleek, satin, reception dress, off the shoulder with a dramatic thigh slit and crystal heels that caught every spotlight.

Reason kissed her hand as they walked. Serenity danced her way in, smiling and laughing. When they reached the dance floor, the DJ let the music ride out while the couple stood in the middle of the floor, dancing.

After the grand entrances, the room settled into a soft, warm rhythm. The lights dimmed to a golden hue, and flickering candles added a soft glow to every table. Guests laughed and passed plates of butter-glazed salmon, buttered shrimp, garlic-roasted chicken, creamy mashed potatoes, grilled asparagus, and buttery rolls. Glasses clinked and toasts were made.

The DJ spun a perfect mix of 90's and 2000's love songs at a low volume. *Fortunate* by Maxwell, *Can You Stand the Rain* by New Edition, and *So Beautiful* by Musiq Soulchild played in the background while people filled their plates and soaked in the beauty of the moment.

Reason leaned over to Serenity, brushing her hand gently as he whispered, "You still real, right? I ain't dream this?"

Serenity smiled, eyes soft. "If you're dreaming, don't wake up."

When dinner ended and the tables had been cleared, the DJ came back on the mic, letting everyone know it was time for the couple's first dance as husband and wife. The room went silent again, except for soft claps, as Reason and Serenity rose from their seats and walked hand in hand to the dance floor. The DJ dropped the lights low and pressed play.

Beyonce's *All Night Long* played. Reason pulled Serenity close, both hands wrapped around her waist. She rested her head against his chest, and the two of them swayed slowly in the middle of the floor, lost in each other like the room had disappeared.

The lyrics were theirs. The night was theirs. And in that moment, nothing existed but the quiet beat of their hearts and the soft hum of a song that felt like it had been written for them. Their family watched with teary smiles. Stephanie wiped her eyes. Vice and Valor nodded quietly. Easton and Scotland sat side by side, grinning from ear to ear. Peaches' portrait, lit by candlelight in the corner of the room, seemed to glow even brighter. And when the song ended, Reason kissed Serenity's forehead then her lips.

The DJ came right back with a vibe, playing Sada Baby's *2k17*. The entire room jumped to their feet, hitting the dance floor. The night turned up in the best way. Uncle Larry two-stepping. Auntie Brenda sliding across the floor in heels too high for her age. Easton doing his version of the worm. Valor and Vice holding court near the bar, surrounded by women. Shayla and Karma dancing barefoot with glow sticks. Even the security guards cracked smiles and nodded to the beat.

It was joy, it was Black love, and it was well earned. And Reason and Serenity? They danced, they laughed, and they loved with the people who meant the most to them in the city that raised them, under the lights of a night that would live in their memory forever.

Epilogue

ONE YEAR LATER

THE MORNING SUN streamed through Reason and Serenity's bedroom windows, casting a soft glow across the sheets as birds chirped gently outside. Serenity stirred, blinking slowly, her hand resting over the swell of her belly. She was exactly one week away from maternity leave, but she wasn't the kind of woman who sat still for long. Reason had tried everything to get her to slow down. He offered to put her on leave early. Hired extra staff at the clinic so that she would work less. Even brought her breakfast in bed for three straight weeks hoping she'd cave, but she never did.

"I'm pregnant, not broken," she told him with a smirk just yesterday.

She sat up, stretching carefully, then moved slowly to the edge of the bed. Her back ached, hips were heavy, but her spirit was light. She showered, rubbed cocoa butter over her belly, and pulled on a set of pink maternity scrubs. She tied her braids into a loose bun, spritzed her neck with Kilian's Love Don't Be Shy, and slid her feet into supportive sneakers.

The drive was short, and when she pulled into the lot, she smiled like she did every morning. Her newly built clinic sat proudly on the corner, double the size of her original one. It was a sleek stone and glass building trimmed with cream and gold signage, a peach-colored flowerbed bordering the walkway.

Inside, the walls were lined with framed photos of former patients, athletes, elderly women and men, as well as kids recovering from surgery. There were private therapy suites, a fully equipped gym, spa recovery rooms, and a kids' rehab space for pediatric clients. Everything about it felt like Serenity, and she couldn't have been happier.

She walked in and greeted her staff – all handpicked, all brilliant. They offered her breakfast, but she declined, opting to eat the fruit bowl she'd brought instead. At 9:00 a.m. sharp, she welcomed her first patient of the day, a middle-aged woman named Denise who was recovering from knee surgery. They moved slowly, focusing on flexibility, small lifts, and walking strength. Serenity guided her gently, encouraging her every step.

"You're doing beautifully," Serenity encouraged, even as a dull ache formed low in her stomach. She paused once to adjust her posture, hand on her hip.

The pain came again, tight and short. She told herself it was Braxton Hicks, knowing she'd been having them for weeks. She brushed it off and continued the session, not missing a beat. She was just finishing up her final notes when another one hit, this time stronger and deeper. She leaned on the counter and exhaled.

"Everything okay, Serenity?" Denise asked, eyes wide.

Serenity forced a smile. "Just the baby stretching."

But the moment she turned toward the hallway, a sudden warm gush soaked her scrubs. She stopped in her tracks, looking down between her legs. Her eyes widened when she realized her water had just broke.

"Oh, shit," she whispered, blinking rapidly. Shane rushed over to Serenity, seeing her leaning against the wall.

"Friend, you good?" he asked, eyes wide.

"My water broke! I'm not even due for another three weeks," Serenity spoke, breathing through the pain.

"Babies don't check calendars!" Shane laughed as he rushed to grab a wheelchair.

As she was wheeled out of the clinic, Serenity grabbed her phone and shakily called the one person she needed in that moment. Reason answered the phone on the first ring.

"You good, baby?"

Her voice cracked into a laugh and a breath all at once. "You might wanna get to the hospital."

"Why?" he asked, already standing and grabbing his keys.

"Because it's time."

Shane sped through the city like it was war time, tires gripping pavement, as Serenity breathed slowly in the passenger seat, gripping the handle and whispering to herself.

"Okay, Shane, not too fast but like kinda fast."

Shane smirked. "Girl, you got a whole human coming out of you. This ain't the time to cruise."

By the time they pulled up to the hospital, Reason was already outside pacing, hoodie half-zipped, looking like he was ready to fight someone and cry at the same time. He rushed to the car the second it stopped and opened Serenity's door.

"Baby, you good?" he asked, breath tight.

Serenity nodded through a deep contraction. "I think this baby is ready to meet us."

"You sure?"

She let out a half-laugh, half-grunt. "It's definitely time."

Reason swept her into his arms, literally picked her up out the car, and carried her inside. Nurses rushed to meet them, guiding them into the delivery suite. The room was softly lit, calm and peaceful, with gentle music playing. It was one of Serenity's favorite songs, *As* by Stevie Wonder. Serenity gripped Reason's hand through every contraction. He never let go, whispering to her, wiping her forehead, rubbing her back between pushes.

"You're almost there. You doing so good, baby. I got you, my baby. Come on, queen. Our baby is almost here."

After hours of labor, sweat, and breathless pain, there was one final push then a cry. The doctor lifted a squirming baby girl into the air, her brown skin glistening under the soft lights, her cry strong and full of fire. They laid her on Serenity's chest, and she broke into tears immediately.

"Hey, baby girl," she whispered. "I've been waiting my whole life to meet you."

Reason stood beside her, eyes wide, lips trembling. He reached down and kissed the top of their daughter's head. Then, he kissed Serenity's hand.

"She's perfect," he whispered. "Just like you."

When the nurse asked what they'd named her, Serenity and Reason looked at each other. They'd talked about a few names, but nothing had stuck. Not until now. Serenity looked down at the tiny bundle in her arms, already calm, already watching the world like she knew it all.

"Her name is Amora Peaches Alexander," she said softly. "Because she came from love, and she carries love with her."

Reason blinked back tears and nodded. "Her grandma would be so honored."

Later that night, Serenity lay in bed, exhausted but glowing. Reason held Amora in the corner chair, rocking gently, shirtless with her laying on his chest. He whispered to her like a prayer.

"Your mama saved me. And now you? You the piece I never knew I needed."

The End....

Did you enjoy the read?
Let us know how much by leaving us a
review on Amazon and Goodreads.

Other Books By
URBAN AINT DEAD

Tales 4rm Da Dale

The Hottest Summer Ever

Hittin' Licks For The Holidays: Atlanta

Wet Dreams On Lockdown: The Nurse

How To Publish A Book From Prison

How To Invest In The Stock Market From Prison

By **Elijah R. Freeman**

Despite The Odds

Despite The Odds 2

By **Juhnell Morgan**

Hittaz

Hittaz 2

Hittaz 3

Hittaz 4

Hittaz 5

Hittaz 6

Coldhearted

Coldhearted 2

Coldhearted 3

By **Lou Garden Price, Sr.**

Wizdom: Forever Your Gangsta

Charge It To The Game

Charge It To The Game 2

Charge It To The Game 3

A Summer To Remember With My Hitta

Snatched Up By A Hitta

Santa Sent Me A Real One For Christmas

Wet Dreams On Lockdown: The Unit Manager

Thug Me The Right Way 2

Thug Me The Right Way 3

Seizing A Gangsta's Heart For The Summer

Yours For The Taking

Wrapped Up In A Hitta's Love For Christmas

By **Nai**

A Set Up For Revenge

A Set Up For Revenge 2

Wet Dreams On Lockdown: The Librarian

By **Ashley Williams**

Trickin' On A Heaux For Christmas

Homie Hoppin' For The Holidays

Wet Dreams On Lockdown: The Female C.O

Letters Of His Love

By **Telia Teanna**

The State's Witness

The State's Witness 2

The State's Witness 3

This Time Won't You Save Me

This Time Won't You Save Me 2

His Summer Side Piece

A Holiday Heist

Healing The Heart Of A Detroit Gangsta

The Promissory

IN The Streetz 4

IN The Streetz 5

By **Tron Hill**

Hittin' Licks For The Holidays: New York

Bandemic

By **Freshh Moneyy**

Coming Soon From
URBAN AINT DEAD

Drill
The Hottest Summer Ever 2
THE G-CODE
Tales 4rm Da Dale 2
How To Build Your Credit From Prison
First Summer Out With My Prison Bae
By **Elijah R. Freeman**

Despite The Odds 3
By **Juhnell Morgan**

A YN'S Muse For The Summer
A Felon's Promise
By **Nai**

The Promissory 2
By **Kyiris Ashley**

Atlantastan 3
By **Chris Green**

IN The Streetz 6
By **Tron Hill**

Bandemic 2
By Freshh Moneyy

9 798990 888296